Ju
F
H65   Hoban, Lillian.
            I met a traveller.

DATE	ISSUED TO

Ju
F
H65   Hoban, Lillian.
            I met a traveller.

Temple Israel Library
Minneapolis, Minn.

Please sign your full name on the above card.

Return books promptly to the Library or Temple Office.

Fines will be charged for overdue books or for damage or loss of same.

I Met A Traveller

An Ursula Nordstrom Book

I Met A Traveller

BY LILLIAN HOBAN

HARPER & ROW, PUBLISHERS
New York, Hagerstown, San Francisco, London

I Met A Traveller
Copyright © 1977 by Lillian Hoban
All rights reserved. No part of this book may be used or reproduced in any manner whatsoever without written permission except in the case of brief quotations embodied in critical articles and reviews. Printed in the United States of America. For information address Harper & Row, Publishers, Inc., 10 East 53rd Street, New York, N.Y. 10022. Published simultaneously in Canada by Fitzhenry & Whiteside Limited, Toronto.
First Edition

Library of Congress Cataloging in Publication Data
Hoban, Lillian.
    I met a traveller.

    "An Ursula Nordstrom book."
    SUMMARY: A young American girl living with her mother in Jerusalem wants to go home.
    [1. Jerusalem—Fiction. 2. Mothers and daughters—Fiction. 3. Single-parent family—Fiction] I. Title.
PZ7.H635Iam   [Fic]   76-58710
ISBN 0-06-022373-1
ISBN 0-06-022374-X lib. bdg.

To the memory of my mother
who was a child in the Second *Aliyah*

I met a traveller from an antique land . . .
PERCY BYSSHE SHELLEY

❧❦❧

I Met A Traveller

❧❦❧

❦

1

❦

My mother's having another affair. This time it's with a creep concert pianist. But that's not so bad. At least he goes away on concert tours, and for a while I get to have things pretty cozy again, like being taken out to dinner and movies and things because she doesn't like to go alone. Her last affair back home in Connecticut was awful. I really suffered and lost a lot of weight. He was a health nut and we never ate anything but brown rice and things like that. He would chew everything seventeen times, and once when I didn't want to eat brown rice and raw fish, and sneaked it under the table to the dog, he got this real hurt expression in his little pale eyes, and said to my mother, "I don't think Josie appreciates what we are doing for her." Only it came out "I don't fink" because he always had a bad cold. The dog got sick.

Finally, the doctor told my mother she ought to take me on a long vacation. She didn't mind, because she and her boyfriend Sheldon were breaking up anyway. What had happened was that Mom and I had spent the whole afternoon going to an organic food store about thirty miles away in upstate Connecticut, the only place where she could get some specially grown sprouted wheat that Sheldon said was essential for his glands. Driving home, we were passing McDonald's, when she spotted Sheldon. He had a Big Mac in each hand, and a thick shake, and a couple of little bags of French fries. He had just stuffed a bite of the Big Mac into his mouth, and was about to follow up with some of the shake when we pulled into the parking lot. Boy! You should have seen his face!

Anyhow, that's how come we live in Jerusalem now. We took this long boat trip, and my mother met this archaeologist who was going to Israel to organize a dig. They really dug each other a lot, and instead of getting off at Greece, we got off at Haifa. The archaeologist disappeared after that, but my mother decided to stay in Israel because, since we're Jewish and all, she said it was really like coming home.

Home used to be a big house in Connecticut. That's when I still had a father. He was kind of neat. He was creative head of a big advertising agency in New York, but what he really wanted to be was a poet. One day he said he needed some time to find himself, and he packed up and left. He found himself a six-foot-tall blonde named Brunhilde and they went to London. They've had two kids in two years, so now I have a couple of half brothers I've never seen. Mom says the kids are bastards because she and Dad never got a divorce.

Sometimes I play this game where I grow up and go to England, and meet one of my long-lost half brothers and we fall in love, and just as we're about to get married someone rushes in and says, "You can't marry each other, you're half brother and sister." And we fall into each other's arms, weeping. But it couldn't really happen, because I am so much older than my half brothers, and girls never get to marry boys younger than they are.

Now that we live in Israel, I spend a lot of time playing games by myself because the school I go to is full of UN Observers' kids and diplomats' kids who don't stay very long, and I never get a chance to make friends. When I grow up I want to be an actress, so it's not really too bad being alone so much. I get a chance to practice my acting. I've written several plays with me taking all the parts, and I get plays out of the library. Last week I got Ibsen's *A Doll's House*, and played the part of Nora. It's a really sad play. The librarian was kind of surprised when I took it out, but I told her it was for my mother, and that the Sam Pig book was for me. Actually they both were. I like to trade off the heavy stuff with something lighter. Like now I'm reading *For Whom the Bell Tolls* with *A Bear Called Paddington*. I prefer Paddington for bedtime reading. It's cozier.

A couple of weeks ago when Boris, the guy Mom's having an affair with, was about to leave on his concert tour, Mom stayed out all night with him. When she got home in the morning to send me off to school, I was crying. There was a mouse in the kitchen making these weird noises that had kept me up all night. I was afraid it was Abu Rauchi, the Arab watchman for the new apartment house they're building across from us. Actually, Abu Rauchi is very nice, and always says "Shalom" and "Keef haleck." But at night if I'm alone, I'm afraid he'll sneak into the house and kill me.

Anyhow, when Mom came home and found me crying she cried a little too, and then she said, "Why don't you write all about it. That way you'll get it out of your system; it will be like therapy." So that's how come I'm writing this. Sort of like the girls who wrote *The Far Distant Oxus*. Only this isn't the Oxus. It's Israel.

2

Today I stayed home from school because I have the flu. I'm glad because I don't like this school, and besides it's nice to stay home sometimes and be with Mom all day. This school is queer, not like the schools in Connecticut I went to. It's a missionary school for converting the heathen. They mean the Jews, I guess. The reason I don't go to a regular Israeli school is because when I first got here I didn't speak any Hebrew, and now that I do, Mom doesn't want to change me over. She says I'm shook up enough, and she doesn't see the sense in shaking me up anymore.

Actually, it's a very pretty school, with a big green iron fence that faces the street. When you walk in the gate you are in a large garden with lots of flowers and trees, and benches to sit on. During break we used to run out of the gate and go to the kiosk up the street. We'd get candy and stuff and bring it back and play in the garden. But now we have a new headmaster and we're not allowed to play in the garden anymore. Now we have to sit in the classroom during break, or play in the little caged area in back of the school.

Mr. Asleson, the new headmaster, is very mean. He lives in the rooms up over the school with his wife and their three kids. He has this funny way of walking sort of sideways really fast like a crab, with his head twisted around over one shoulder so he's looking backwards. He keeps his mouth open all the time and he does this awful thing with his tongue going round and round to wet his chapped lips. His daughter Catherine is in my class. She is not allowed out of the school compound. Once, when one of the girls had a birthday party and invited all the girls in the class to come, he wouldn't let her go. She threw herself on the floor and kicked her heels and cried, but he still wouldn't let her go. I'm glad he's not my father; it must be rotten to have a father who's a missionary and gets sent all over to convert the heathen.

We sing some really far-out hymns in assembly every morning, then we have morning prayers, then we have classes. I'm pretty good in English composition and Scripture, but the teacher told my mother that my Maths were shocking. For extracurricular I chose drama, and I got to be Potiphar's wife in *Joseph and His Technicolor Dream Coat*. I liked playing the part of a wanton woman. Everyone thought it was really funny when I threw the rose that I was supposed to throw disdainfully at Joseph when he refused my advances and it landed right in Mr. Asleson's lap.

In the winter we have to wear our overcoats in school, and even then we freeze. It's not as though it gets that lovely crisp cold, like in Connecticut. It just is raw and it rains all the time, and the walls are made of stone and get damp and cold and moldy. There's a big old stove in the classroom, but most of the time it doesn't work. Or if it does, it explodes and shoots soot all over the place. Once, last winter, the stove in our classroom exploded and the smokestack fell down. There was such a crash that everyone thought we had been infiltrated by terrorists. No one thought it was a bomb though. Once you've heard a bomb go off, you never mistake anything else for it.

Last year during the Yom Kippur War there was no school. Mom and I put canned stuff and water and candles down in our shelter, and painted the headlights of our car dark blue, leaving only a tiny hole for the light to shine through. It looked so eerie at night; all the houses blacked out, all the streets pitch black, except here and there tiny little pinpoints of light where a car was moving.

Most of the men were gone, and the women and young boys took over delivering milk and bread and things to the grocery stores. Mom and I volunteered to deliver telegrams. We had a great time together, especially since that creep Boris had been called up for duty. We'd leave early in the morning, pick up a batch of telegrams and cables at the post office, and spend the rest of the day

9

trying to find the addresses. It was hot, sweaty work, but we felt good because we were helping out in the war.

"Excuse me, Geverit," I said one day after having spent an hour trying to locate a Miss Cindy Arnold. "Do you know where this address is?"

The woman was patiently waiting her turn to get into the supermarket. The war brought out the best in people; everyone, very gentle and polite, waited in line for bread almost cheerfully. She looked at the name on the cable I was holding.

"Raquel," she called to a woman at the front of the line. "You know that little blonde American girl, the one who's been going with your nephew's friend? Here's a cable for her."

Raquel motioned for Mom and me to come over.

"Is it important?" she asked Mom.

"How should I know," Mom answered.

"Well, if it's not so important, the next time my daughter-in-law comes to my house, I'll get her to bring it to Cindy."

"We're supposed to deliver it to her," Mom said.

"O.K." Raquel shrugged her shoulders. "If you want to go all the way to Ramat Gan, it's not my business. But that's where she lives now. She moved last week, right next door to my daughter-in-law."

"Maybe it's not very important," I whispered to Mom. "Maybe we should let her give it to her daughter-in-law."

"Listen," said Raquel. "What could it hurt if you read it? That way you'll know. Then, if it's really important,

I'll call up my daughter-in-law, and she'll right away tell Cindy what it says."

Mom hesitated a minute, then she opened the cable. CINDY COME HOME IMMEDIATELY, it said, MOTHER FRANTIC ABOUT YOUR SAFETY. CAN RETURN TO ISRAEL WHEN WAR IS OVER.

I looked at the cables we still had to deliver. "Look," I said to Mom. "All American names: Richard Arliss, Andrew Saunders, Geoffrey Shaw, Linda Coleman. Probably from parents begging their kids to come home. Do you think it really is dangerous here now?" I asked.

"Shh!" Mom said. Someone in the line had turned on a transistor radio, and everyone was silent, avidly listening to the news broadcast. People walking past stopped and listened; it was the first week of the war, and the news was very grave.

As we drove home that afternoon, I asked Mom again, "Do you think we really are in danger?" The sky overhead was blue and cloudless and no one seemed afraid. Only Abu Rauchi had disappeared. I guess he thought Jerusalem would be bombed, because he was always listening to broadcasts from Egypt on his little transistor radio, but until today, it had all felt perfectly safe.

"I thought about it just once when the war started, Josie," Mom said. "We couldn't leave. It wouldn't be right even if it were dangerous."

"You mean we would stay here even if you thought we might get killed?" I asked.

"Look Josie. You don't run out on people you love at

the first sign of unpleasantness or danger."

"You mean you love Boris more than you love me. You don't even care if I'm in danger or not."

"Now you listen to me! I guess because I talk to you as though you're grown up, I forget you really can't understand some of the things I tell you. And you think it gives you license to be snotty. You and I are not talking about the same kind of love. I love these people, Josie, and I'm going to stand by them. Can't you understand loyalty?"

Mom's voice had begun to shake. There was a low rumble of artillery on the Bika, the long valley road that leads to the Galilee, and the answer that was on the tip of my tongue stayed put.

That night, when the drone of the helicopters bringing the wounded soldiers from the Sinai to Hadassah Hospital woke me, I thought I heard another sound as well. I got out of bed and tiptoed the length of the hallway on the cool tiles to Mom's room. She was standing at the window, leaning her arms on the marble sill, her face lifted to the sound of the copters, tears running down her cheeks.

I didn't say any more about it being dangerous after that, not even on the day I came in and found Mom holding a cable of our own.

"Your father wants to evacuate you," she said looking at me, her expression not telling me a thing. "Do you want to go?"

"No," I answered. And that was that.

But that was then, and this is now. Lying here in bed

sick, I can think of lots of reasons why I want to leave Israel. Take school for instance. What I really don't like about school is that all the girls in my class except Catherine and me wear bras and have their period. Catherine doesn't count though. She wears an undershirt and long drawers even when it's khamsin, and the hot hot wind blows and blows until everyone is ready to jump out of his skin. But no one bothers her. She's so queer anyway, that she would probably say the Lord Jesus wants her to wear an undershirt and long drawers.

That leaves me. I'm much smaller than any of the other girls even though I'm only the youngest by four months. When all the other girls get together and whisper about things, I usually sit by myself and make believe I don't care. They brag about being black and blue from the boys snapping their bras in the back, and they show off their cute bikini underpants. One of the girls has a pair with a big mouth embroidered on them that says Kiss Me Here Baby! Everyone thinks it's really neat the way she has a tiny American flag pinned up over the mouth.

This morning, when Mom brought me my breakfast in bed, I said to her, "Do you think when I'm better we could go downtown and see if maybe one of the stores has a bra that might fit me?"

Mom put down the tray and rumpled my hair. "You've got nothing to put in a bra, baby. You ought to be glad that you aren't all grown up. Those girls in your class that are so developed will probably look like old frumps by the time they're thirty-five. I know it's kind of hard to live through the undershirt syndrome, but you wait and see; you'll be thankful when you're older."

I guess she's right. Sometimes when I think about it, it does seem nice. I mean, people are children for such a short time. They spend most of their lives being grown up and getting old, so it is kind of nice that I'm allowed a little extra childhood. But most of the time, all it means is getting left out of everything.

This afternoon, when I felt better, I sat by the window and watched some new people move into the building where Abu Rauchi is the watchman. Abu Rauchi came back as soon as the war was over. He showed up one evening as usual, smiling and bowing, and brought us a cumcum of coffee the way he always does. He was salaaming to the new people now, in a friendly, interested way.

They were Russian immigrants, you could tell, because they had so few things to move. There was a plump old lady with rosy cheeks and two silver teeth in the front. There are lots of new Russian immigrants in Israel, and most of them have a lot of gold teeth, but this old lady had silver ones. She was carrying an accordian, and she stood out in the street and directed the movers who were hauling the bed and table and boxes out of the truck. Her husband was in a wheelchair, and he looked awfully thin and gray. Every once in a while, she would bend over him and wipe his face very gently, and once when she straightened up, she looked over at me. When she saw me in the window, she smiled; that's when I saw her silver teeth.

It must be awful to leave the country where you were

born and know you can never go back. I would die if I knew I would never see America again. I dream about America at night sometimes. I dream I'm back in my own house, and going to a good plain normal American school. What I really really want most in the world is to go back to the United States.

3

The ambulance came the other night, and they took Mr. Yanovitch, the Russian lady's husband, to the hospital. Everyone stood around on the street and watched while they carried him out on a stretcher. He is all skin and bones, and he looked pitiful under the sheet they had covering him. I guess Mrs. Yanovitch will be staying at the hospital most of the time, so I won't be seeing much of her.

The day after they moved in, she waved to me when she came out to go shopping in the morning. I was still home sick, although my temperature was down, and my bed is right next to the window, so I can see everything that is happening on the street. She came out of her apartment house and nodded and smiled at Abu Rauchi. He salaamed to her. You could tell that they liked each other even though they couldn't talk. She had one of those plastic shopping bags so I knew she was going to the little grocery store, the makolet, down the street. I waved back at her, although that isn't the type of thing I usually do. I mean I'm usually pretty careful not to give people the idea that just because I'm little they can get familiar with me. But she had such a nice way of smiling with her silver teeth shining in the sunlight, that I couldn't help smiling and waving back.

When she came back from the makolet, she walked right to my window, and reached up and gave me a chocolate bar. She's round and plump and not terribly tall, and she had to stand on her tiptoes even though my window is practically street level. I said, "Thank you," and took it, because I didn't know what else to do. A little dog had followed her across the street, and she pointed to it and said, "Sabatchka," and smiled.

I repeated it after her slowly, "sa-ba-tch-ka."

She nodded her head emphatically, and said, "Da," and laughed. That afternoon, she wheeled her husband out on their little balcony and played the accordian for him. He seemed to enjoy it and even kept time with one bony finger, but then he had a terrible coughing fit, and she wheeled him into the house again.

My mother found out from the makolet keeper that they don't have any friends or family here, and they can't speak anything but Russian. The makolet keeper is Rumanian, which means he can speak just about any language, and he and Mrs. Yanovitch get along fine. She told him that Mr. Yanovitch has cancer of the lungs, and wanted to be able to breathe free air again before he dies. They used to be actors in Russia, and were pretty happy there. But one time their whole troupe of actors and musicians and acrobats were allowed to accept an invitation to perform in another country, and once Mr. Yanovitch had breathed free air, he knew he couldn't be happy in Russia anymore. As soon as he got sick, they applied for visas to come to Israel. They didn't have to wait as long as most Jews do, because the Russians didn't mind letting Mr. Yanovitch go, now that he is sick.

Things are very hard for them here in Israel, even though the Absorption Agency helps them with money and gave them an apartment and everything. It would be different if either of them could work, or even if they could speak Hebrew. But with Mr. Yanovitch so sick, and Mrs. Yanovitch taking care of him, there's not much they can do.

I watched Mom paint all morning after Mrs. Yanovitch gave me the candy bar. Mom's an artist, and sends her paintings back to a New York gallery to sell.

"Well, what do you think, Josie," she said. "Do you think they'll like this new one?"

"It's awfully big, isn't it?" I asked. She was doing a view from our living-room window; part of the Old City, and the little Arab village, and all the hills beyond. The canvas was so huge that she sort of had to skip around to cover it with her little nervous dabs of paint.

"If they paid by the square inch, I'd really do all right on this." She sighed. "We could use the money." She turned and looked at me. "You know," she said, "sometimes I think it's not so much that I'm a liberated woman, it's that I've liberated a man. Liberated your father from any responsibility for you. Pretty cute, huh?"

She laughed, as though she'd just made a very funny joke. I didn't think it was so funny, but I laughed anyway. I know she's proud of the fact that she supports us, and never gets any money from Dad. Mom and I get along pretty well, especially when she's not having an affair. Or like now, when Boris is in Europe on his concert tour, and she stays home most of the time.

But when he's around, it's pretty rotten. We eat dinner real fast, food just slapped down on the table in the pot it was cooked in, the butter still in its paper wrapper without benefit of a dish; not exactly company. Then Mom says, "Why don't you clear the table, and do your homework and hop into bed. I'll come and tuck you in when I get home." She runs upstairs, and puts on something pretty so she'll look nice for Boris, and leaves, blowing me a kiss from the door.

Tucking me in is a leftover from when I was a baby. Mom and Dad both used to come up when I was in bed, and tuck the blankets around me all cozy and warm and kiss me good night. Now I get tucked in anytime she gets home, even though I've been asleep for hours. I generally check with her in the morning, just to make sure she remembered to do it.

I clear the table, if I feel like it, and do my homework, and sit around by myself. If I were in Connecticut, I'd be able to call my friends, or watch TV or something. The best thing on Israeli TV is *Ironside,* on Saturday night. I mean that really is a big deal. I hardly even ever watched that in the US. Jordan TV isn't too bad, if you can get it. But most of the time the reception is awful. So I read, or make up plays to act out. Then, about eleven o'clock, I put myself to bed. But first I call the wake-up service or I wouldn't be able to get up in the morning. The alarm doesn't wake either me or Mom. Especially if she's been out late with Boris.

When I got over the flu and went back to school, I hated it more than ever. I missed a couple of tests when I was sick, and I am so far behind in Math it isn't even funny. The girls ignore me just as much as ever. They sort of lump me in with Catherine, as though we were both the same kind of queers. The first day I went back, I was so depressed I almost cried. All the way home on the bus I kept pretending it was the school bus back home in Connecticut, and all my friends were on it, and the driver was Sperry, who has long hair and wears one earring and tells jokes to the kids. But the fact is, it was an Egged bus, and the people on it were pushing and shoving and picking their noses.

The last three stops before I got off, I spent in my usual sweat, trying to figure out how I was going to pull the cord that signals the driver to stop. I'm too small to reach it, and it's embarrassing to have to ask someone to do it for me. This time I was lucky. Some woman was getting off at my stop, and she pulled it.

When I got off the bus, I ran all the way home; past empty houses bombed out in one of the wars, across the weed-grown lot with its rusty barbed wire and old trash, and up the hill next to the convent wall. Mom was out, and I let myself in with the key I wear around my neck. I threw the shopping bag with my books in it down on the floor right there in the hall, and went into my room and lay down on the bed. My old teddy bear was sitting propped up against the pillow, and I pulled him over and hugged him. "Teddy," I said, "I hate it here!" There's no use telling Mom how unhappy I am, and how much I hate it. I've told her lots of times.

"Oh no," she said the first time I begged her to go home. "I'm not moving back. There's no way I'm going to become a suburban hausfrau again, constantly schlepping you around in the car. I love it here Josie—love all the marvelously interesting people, all the great concerts. And the light! It's perfect for painting! But mostly, I love the quality of life. Josie, you don't understand. Jerusalem is practically the ideal combination of small town and big city." She was arranging fruit in a bowl, and she stopped and turned to me. "Look," she said, "just something as simple as these apples. I sent you downtown to get them, and I didn't have to worry about you. You can take a bus and be perfectly safe. I'd think twice about sending you downtown alone if we lived in an American city."

"Yeah," I said. "Sure. It's safe for me to take a bus here by myself. I can take a bus and go to the movies by myself, I can take a bus and go to the library by myself, I can take a bus and go into town and shop in the department store by myself. I hate it!"

"Well, make some friends! That way you won't have to do things by yourself." And that was the way we usually ended the conversation.

I rubbed my nose against Teddy's. "You're my friend aren't you, Teddy?" I said. After a while, I got up and put on my roller skates. Roller skating always makes me feel good. I went out and skated up and down the street, singing "Little Lambs Love Jesus" and "I Don't Care If It Rains or Freezes I Am Safe in the Arms of Jesus," scandalizing all the people around who could understand English, and I was beginning to feel much better. Then Mrs. Yanovitch came out on her balcony and waved to me, and motioned for me to come up.

I took off my roller skates, and went into her apartment building. Most of it is still unfinished, and there are bags of cement and all kinds of tools lying around in the front entrance. It has a dank kind of bomb-shelter smell. They are the only people who live there, so it wasn't too hard to find their door. I was surprised at how nice she had fixed their place up. She has pictures of herself and her husband and the troupe they used to be with up on the walls, and she has a samovar on the table with an embroidered cloth under it.

She had baked something that looked like little chocolate macaroons, and she had them on a plate on the table. There were two teacups and some slices of lemon and some jam on the table too. She smiled and offered me the chocolate macaroony things, and poured me a cup of tea. Mr. Yanovitch must have been asleep in the other room, because I never saw him. I said, "Thank you," to her, and drank the tea and ate the cake.

She pointed to the table and said something that

sounded like "Chtow eto." I thought she meant table, so I said "table." After a while, when she pointed to quite a few things and said, "Chtow eto," I could see it meant, "What is this?" I taught her how to say table and chair and girl in English, but it wasn't much of a conversation. Mostly we just sat and smiled at each other. Then she brought out her accordian and played and sang a Russian song softly so as not to wake up Mr. Yanovitch. "I-vu-sh-ka Ze-le-na-ya," she sang. It was very nice, kind of sad and dreamy. I went home after that.

$$\approx\!\S\!\approx$$

4

$$\approx\!\S\!\approx$$

That awful boy, Mathias Glauter, oh how I hate him! Before I got sick, he used to bother me when he had nothing better to do during recess. He would come up to me all nasty and greasy looking with an ugly smile on his face. "You love me. Why do you love me?" he'd drag out slowly while he gave me an excruciating little Indian pinch. He has a German accent and he always sounds mean, but when he says, "Why do you love me?" like that it makes my blood run cold. I try to ignore him and usually I walk away. But since I've come back to school he's been really awful.

Today, he came up in back of me and kicked me, a sharp fast little kick so that nobody saw him do it, and when I let out a yell, he said, "You are crying because you love me, yes?" Some of the kids came over and stood around, and he turned to them and said, "She loves me, and I don't want it," in that slow draggy way.

Catherine said, "She doesn't love you, Mathias. You're just being mean to her because you hate Jews."

Mathias pulled himself up very straight and clenched his fists. "Jesus was a Jew," he said, staring very hard at Catherine. "My father says it is our duty to love Jews." Mathias's father is a missionary, and they only came here a few months ago.

"Yeah, sure," said Maryanne. *"Roses are red, And violets are blue, But whatever you do, Don't marry a Jew."* Maryanne is kind of cute. Her father's with the UN and they come from England. Actually, she and I are pretty friendly. We eat lunch together when Stella doesn't come to school. Stella and Maryanne are best friends, and they always do everything together.

I think it made Mathias mad to have the other kids stick up for me, and that's one of the reasons I never hit him back, or tell any of the teachers when he pinches me. If I get him mad, he'll just be that much meaner. But I'd never tell any of the teachers anyway. There's a girl in my class who's about five foot nine, and she's forever going up to Mrs. Farrell and whimpering like a baby. Anytime anyone so much as looks cross-eyed at her, she runs to teacher. I could never do that.

After recess, we have Math. Our Math teacher, Mr. Vandervoss, is from Holland, and his English is worse than Mathias's. He gets terribly angry because we can't understand him. Every once in a while he works himself up into a regular frenzy and throws all his books and papers on the floor and says he won't teach us anymore.

I have a terrible time with Math anyway, and having him for a teacher hasn't helped much. Sometimes, if I really can't understand what we're supposed to be doing, I'll go up to him and try to get him to explain, and he's not so bad. He'll say, "But you moost try, you moost try." His breath smells like rotten eggs.

Today, I decided to ask Mr. Vandervoss to explain how to do one of the problems he'd given us for homework. I have to pass Mathias's desk to get to the front of the room, and just as I walked past, he whipped out a little steel ruler he had hidden under his desk, and hit me on the back of the knee. At the same time, he let out an awful scream.

"She hit me, she hit me!" he yelled.

Mr. Vandervoss's face turned red and he squinted up his eyes till they were like slits.

"Joosie," he hissed at me, "you sit down now." He paused between each word as though he could hardly make the sounds come out through his clenched teeth. I really was scared. But the back of my knee where Mathias had hit me stung like crazy, and just this once, I wanted to tell on him.

"Mathias hit me, Mr. Vandervoss. He hit me with a steel ruler."

"She lies, she lies!" screamed Mathias, and he actually made tears come out of his eyes.

Mr. Vandervoss came down the aisle and grabbed me by the arm, and shoved me back to my seat. "Joosie," he said, breathing rotten eggs all over me, "you have now detention one hour after school."

By the time I got home, an hour late because of the detention, the back of my knee was black and blue. Mom met me at the door. "I was worried about you. How come you're home so late?"

I told her about Mathias and Mr. Vandervoss.

"Oh God," she said. "Josie, you've got to think of something more believable than that."

"What do you mean?" I asked her.

"You're not going to try to tell me that this kid is anti-Semitic just because he's German," she said. "It's just not possible anymore."

"I'm not trying to tell you anything except what happened. You're just like Mr. Vandervoss. He didn't believe me either."

"I'm not saying Mathias didn't hit you. I'm just saying that you've got the reason all wrong. Are you sure you don't do something to provoke him?"

"Yeah, Mom. Standing around during recess, or passing his desk provokes him. Oh what's the difference, you don't care what happens to me."

"Josie, you know that's not true. Why don't you tell Mrs. Farrell or some other teacher who speaks English if someone is persecuting you?"

"Because I don't like to rat on other kids, that's why."

"Well, I suppose if it happens again, I'll have to go in and talk to Mrs. Farrell." The phone rang, and she sighed and went to answer it.

I went outside and sat on the step. Mrs. Yanovitch was walking slowly up the hill next to the convent wall, coming home from seeing Mr. Yanovitch at the hospital.

When she saw me, she waved to me and beckoned. I walked across the street and we went up to her apartment. Before Mr. Yanovitch was taken to the hospital, I used to go over quite often to have tea and listen to Mrs. Yanovitch play the accordian. But now, I don't see her quite as much, and I sort of miss it. By now, I know the names of all the actors and actresses in the pictures on her wall, and I've told her a lot about myself, not that she understands most of what I'm saying.

I told her about Mathias and showed her the bruise on the back of my knee. She made a lot of little chirping noises, and made me lie down on the bed. Then she wrung a towel out in cold water, and put it on the bruise while she made some tea. I love to watch Mrs. Yanovitch drink tea. She puts part of a cube of sugar in her mouth, and sucks the tea up through it, sort of inhaling the tea through the sugar. She always puts a spoonful of strawberry preserves in my cup, and I spoon the preserves up a little at a time, sipping tea through strawberries.

After we had our tea, she took a teaspoon and put it in the freezer. When it got good and cold, she pressed it up against the back of my knee, and the bruise didn't feel sore anymore. We sat together until it was almost dark and Mrs. Yanovitch had to go back to the hospital again.

❦❦❦

5

❦❦❦

$\mathcal{M}$r. Yanovitch died at the end of the month. They buried him the next day. I asked Mom if I could go to the funeral, because I knew Mira, that's Mrs. Yanovitch, would be all alone.

"What do you want to do that for?" Mom asked. "Sounds pretty ghoulish for an eleven-year-old to want to go to a funeral."

"I just want to go," I said.

"Well, you can't stay out of school. You've been out entirely too much."

"If it's after school can I go?" I was just asking to find out how she felt about me going, because I knew that the funeral was at ten in the morning, and I knew I would go no matter what she said. But to tell the truth, I was a little scared. I mean I'd never seen a dead person.

Mom stopped painting and looked at me. "You really

like Mrs. Yanovitch a lot," she said.

"She's nice to me. She's teaching me how to play the accordian. Anyway, I'm the only person who visits her."

I had gotten into the habit, ever since the day Mathias had hit me with the steel ruler, of stopping off on my way home from school and having tea with Mira. And she made sure to be home when I got there. Even though Mr. Yanovitch was in the hospital, she came home in time to give me tea in the afternoon. Then she would go back again in the evening.

Mom looked thoughtful, then she said, "Tell you what, Josie, why don't we have her over for dinner tomorrow night?"

"She won't be able to come, Mom. She has to sit shiva and all."

"I didn't know she was religious," Mom said.

"She isn't, but the rabbi kind of laid it on her that she had to."

"Well, maybe we can make dinner and bring it over to her. Make a cake, too." Mom can be really nice sometimes. I didn't say anything more about going to the funeral.

The next day, I left at the usual time, as though I were going to school. But I went over to Mira's house instead. We waited at her house until nine thirty to take the bus to the place where the service would be held. Mira didn't cry or anything. She just sat very quietly, her hands folded in her lap, waiting to go.

We got to the place before ten, and had to wait. It looked a little like a chapel. There was a courtyard with plants, and inside the building, off a corridor, there were a couple of small rooms. Mr. Yanovitch was lying on a stretcher in one of the rooms, exactly the way they had brought him from the hospital. He was wrapped up in a sheet, just lying there. No coffin, no flowers, nothing. That is the way they bury people here. Without a coffin, without flowers, without any pretending that it's anything but a dead body that's going into the bare ground.

Mira started crying when she saw him. It was pretty awful. Him just lying there wrapped in a sheet. You knew right away they hadn't bothered to spare any clothes and be wasteful; that underneath the sheet he was naked. I wasn't really scared. I just wished there was a coffin, and I wished there were flowers and music. Most of all I wished that I could pretend that Mr. Yanovitch wasn't really there under the sheet, all small and gray and dead.

After a while, some men dressed in black, with wide-brimmed hats, showed up. They did a little praying and chanting, and then they covered Mr. Yanovitch with a prayer shawl and they carried the stretcher out into the courtyard. As they came out of the door, they broke a glass on the stone walk, and the sound rang out loud and clear. I knew they always broke a glass at weddings, but I had never heard of breaking one when someone died.

The rabbi prayed a little out in the courtyard, with the sun coming down hot and bright and everyone sweating. They passed around a bottle of orangeade and some paper cups, and swayed and chanted some more. Then they loaded the stretcher into a police wagon, and the professional mourners held out a little brass cup with a neat little handle, and shook it so we could hear the coins clinking inside. Mira put some money in, and then she and I got into the police wagon with the stretcher and Mr. Yanovitch on it. The mourners got in too.

We took the road out toward Tel Aviv, past the Paz gas station, and turned off to the left up a hill. Most of the way out, I tried not to look at the stretcher, but it was kind of hard because my knees were bumping up against it, right where Mr. Yanovitch's feet made two mounds under the prayer shawl. The road wound around for quite a while, and then it became a rutted dirt road. The police wagon rattled along, raising clouds of grayish white dust that settled on the broad-brimmed black hats of the mourners, and all over the prayer shawl that Mr. Yano-vitch was covered with, and all over Mira and me.

Finally, we stopped. The mourners carried the stretcher over to a shallow trench in the gray white ground. Mira and I followed, stumbling over new graves that were marked only with little sticks. Then some of the mourn-ers heaved the stretcher over on its side, and kind of shook Mr. Yanovitch off into the shallow trench that was his grave, pulling the prayer shawl off him at the same time. One of the mourners folded up the prayer shawl carelessly, and stuck it under his arm, ready for the next one, I guess. I couldn't help noticing the dried old blood stain on one corner of it, and I shivered even though it was dreadfully hot.

They were shoveling the pale gray dirt in over Mr. Yanovitch. Mira started to scream, and put her hands up to cover her eyes. I held her around the waist. My arm didn't really go very far around her. Clouds of flies were coming out of a crack in the dried earth of a new grave that we were standing near, and they settled on our faces and lips and eyelids. I kept thinking of where they had been before they settled on my dried-out lips, and brushing them away in absolute horror, but they were very persistent. I guess they liked live flesh better than dead. After the rabbi had said a few more words over Mr. Yanovitch's grave, and everyone had had some more orangeade, we all piled into the police wagon and drove back to Jerusalem.

Luckily, Mom was not home. As soon as I got into the house I took all my clothes off as fast as I could, and threw them in the dirty-clothes basket. Then I stood in the shower and let the water just stream down me. I washed my hair even though I had washed it the day before. When I was head to toe perfectly clean, I stood there in the shower with my face up, and opened my mouth, and let the water run in and pour out again. I just couldn't rid myself of the feeling of gray white dust that had settled in my hair in my eyebrows in my mouth on my teeth.

≈❦≈

6

≈❦≈

$\mathcal{E}$very night that week I dreamt the same dream. I dreamt that I was being buried in a shallow trench. They were shoveling hot gray-white dirt in on top of me and it got in my nose and my mouth and I couldn't breathe or scream. The smell of the earth was awful, a sick sweet hot dank smell that I could taste. When I'd wake up in the morning I'd know that somehow I had to get back to Connecticut. Back to all the normal things I love. The feel of the rich brown dirt squooshing between my toes when I walk down near the pond in the summer. The apple-crisp tang of the autumn air. The smell of smoke drifting across the fields when old man Krieger burns leaves. Ice skating, snow, all of it.

I tried to tell Mom about it at breakfast one morning.

"I know how you feel, Jo-Jo baby, but when you grow up you'll thank me for this experience. You'll know how lucky you are to be living here now," Mom said. She pushed down the plunger in the French coffee pot and brought it over to the table. I played with my pancakes, shoving them around on the plate. It was Saturday, and there would be nothing to do all day again. No buses, no movies, nothing open. A lump rose in my throat and I was afraid I was going to cry.

"Please let me go home, Mom. I bet Erin's mother would be glad to have me stay with them. That way she wouldn't have to drive Erin around to friends' houses all the time. She'd have me to play with. Please Mom, I hate it here."

"Look Josie," Mom said, her lips getting that narrow tight look they get when she's unhappy. "We've been through all this. Connecticut is a great place for kids, it's a great place for families, but it's a rotten place for ME. There's no way I'm going to live in the suburbs again. I'm sick of being just one more single woman that no one invites to anything but coffee klatches. Sorry baby, I'm happy here, and as long as you're a little girl you stay with me."

What she really meant was that she cared more about Boris than she did about me. There had been a letter from him the day before from London. It seemed odd that he should be playing a concert in the city my father lives in. I wondered if my father had gone to the concert. If he knew when Boris walked across the stage and bowed, and lifted his tails and sat down to play, that that was Mom's lover. I wondered if Brunhilde went to the concert with my father. Suddenly I got a funny twisted feeling in my head. All these people were weaving around my brain. In and out, in and out. Like skeins of thread making all kinds of crazy tangled patterns. But I wasn't in the patterns. Nowhere in my head was there room for me.

"What do you want to do today, go on a picnic?" Mom had started to wash up, clattering and banging the dishes in that sun-dazzled Saturday morning in Jerusalem silence.

"No, I think I'll go over to Mira's for a while." I walked out on the balcony, and looked at the hills. You can see the little Arab village, Silwan, and the wadi that it slopes down to, and part of the Old City with the Dome of the Rock and El Aqsa and above that the Mount of Olives and Mount Scopus, and away in the distance, way beyond the Judean hills, a dark pinkish-gray smudge, the mountains of Jordan. Oh, it was beautiful, all right. But it gave me the same twisted feeling. Like the skeins of thread that were Boris and Brunhilde and Mom and Dad. It didn't have me in it anywhere.

I got dressed and walked across the street to Mira's. Abu Rauchi salaamed and said, "Keef haleck." It was hot, hot, khamsin hot, even though it was almost winter.

"Douzhynka," Mira said when she answered the door. Her whole face lights up when she smiles that silver-toothed smile. She was teaching me a Russian song about a tree wrapped in snow and frost, and she brought out her accordian and started to play it softly. Tears came into her eyes, and I could tell she wasn't just crying because Mr. Yanovitch had died. She was crying because she missed Russia. She missed the snow and the cold and the ice, just as much as I missed Connecticut.

Once she said to me, "Ya lyoublyou snegh. Ya lyoublyou snegh vh gorodye." "I love snow. I love snow in the city." She had a faraway, wistful look in her eyes that made me think of the story of the snow queen and the ice palace, and Kay, the little boy who got the splinter of glass in his eye and in his heart. I had given her a paperweight that my father gave me years ago when he came back from a trip that the advertising agency had sent him on. It is made of clear plastic, kind of dome shaped, and it has little houses and trees inside. When you shake it, it snows all over the houses and the trees, and it looks like a city in a snow storm. Mira loves it.

We sat there, feeling sad together, Mira playing the notes on the accordian very softly. It wasn't quite as bad as feeling sad alone. I began to get an idea in my head, and the more I thought about it, the more sense it made.

"Mira," I said, "let's go to America. Just you and me." As soon as the words came out of my mouth, I felt good. Mira kept playing the accordian, and nodded and smiled the way she always does when I talk to her. I talk to her an awful lot, even though she can't understand most of it. Usually it doesn't matter too much. But now, it really did.

"Mira," I said slowly. "You," I pointed to her, "me," I pointed to myself, "AMERICA!" I was practically shouting. She stopped playing the accordian and looked at me.

"Do you understand, Mira? Do you understand? America! You and me!"

"Ameryka?" Mira asked. She lifted her palms, and shrugged her shoulders.

I started thinking out loud, now, the way I often did with her. "Mira," I said, "listen to me. You know that two hundred dollars I have?" I had it stashed away in the back of my bureau drawer where Aida, the Arab maid, wouldn't find it. It was in crisp new hundred-dollar bills. My father had sent it to me for my last birthday, the only time I ever heard from him. He had sent it with a letter.

"Dear Josie, Last night I saw John Gielgud in a scintillatingly witty production. The night before, I was fortunate enough to be present when Nicol Williamson performed in what must have been the quintessential *Hamlet*. On the weekend we (Brunhilde and I) went to a charming bit of fluff at the Little Angel Marionette Theatre. If you really want to be an actress, London would offer you such versatility! It would be as meat and drink to you! Perhaps you could use the enclosed money to come visit. Love, Dad."

That was on my eleventh birthday, written on the bright yellow paper Dad favors. Mom almost exploded when I showed it to her.

"My God! Doesn't he know how old you are? This sounds like he wants it preserved for posterity, not like a letter a father writes to his daughter on her eleventh birthday! And that yellow paper! Like the yellow slick in *The Caine Mutiny*."

She told Boris about it when she thought I couldn't hear. I remember squirming inwardly; it wasn't bad enough that Dad didn't really care enough about me to write a real letter. Anyway, there was something pathetic about it. As though he couldn't find words anymore to tell me how he felt. Or maybe he had lost touch with his feelings so there was an emptiness that could only be filled in with silly bright fancy-sounding words.

I didn't answer the letter. I mean what could I say. "Dear Dad, This is me, *me*, your quintessential daughter. Remember? The kid you used to carry piggyback?"

I didn't know what to do with the money when I got it. It was too much to go out and spend all at once. But if I just bought little things every once in a while, it would melt away, and I wouldn't even feel as though I had gotten a birthday present at all. So I had kept it. And I still had it. And Mira and I would get the rest somehow, so we could go to America together!

"I'll fix it up with Mom, Mira. You don't have to worry about that. But it might be a good idea if we don't say anything to her about it just yet." I didn't know exactly how I was going to fix it up, but now that I had decided that Mira and I were going to America together, I felt so good about everything, that nothing seemed too hard to do. "Tomorrow I'll go to a travel agency and find out how much tickets cost. Oh Mira, Mira, I can't wait! I can't wait!" I got up and hugged her, accordian and all, and did a little dance. She looked pleased by the hug, but kind of puzzled. I wished that I could make her understand, make her want to go.

"You wait till you see it, Mira. You'll love it. Look, I have pictures of me and our house and the pond and all, that Dad took after the big snow we had a couple of years ago. I'll run home and get them."

Mom was upstairs painting, and she called down to me

when she heard the door slam. "How is Mira, sweetie, is she doing all right?"

"She's O.K., Mom. I'm going back over. I just came home to get something."

"Well, be home in time for lunch. Dina and Gideon are coming over, and we'll probably go for a drive down to the Dead Sea afterwards. Do you think Mira would like to come?"

"I don't know, Mom. I don't think she'd be allowed to, while she's sitting shiva." Actually Mira wasn't sitting shiva anymore, but I wasn't too anxious for the two of them to get together right then. I knew Mira hadn't understood most of what I had said. But somehow, she and I had something together now that we didn't have before. And in a way, it was against Mom.

I got my photo album and went back to Mira's. We spread the pictures that weren't glued into the album out on the table. There were some of me sledding, and some of me with my dog Foster in front of the kitchen where I had built a huge snowman. There were some of old man Krieger sweeping the pond below our house with his snow plow. If you look real close you can see me ice skating on the path he's just cleared. And there were some of me making angels in the snow.

"Chtow eto?" asked Mira, pointing to the one that showed me and Foster in front of our kitchen.

"That's our house, Mira. House." I pointed to her little kitchen, then back to the picture. "Mine. My house."

"Horoshow," said Mira.

"Yes," I said. "And no one lives in it now. It's been

up for sale since we came here, but no one has bought it yet. All our furniture is still in it, and most of my books, and even some of my toys." You could see in through the sliding-glass door of the kitchen. The picture was in color, so all the French pots and pans and baskets hanging from the hood over the stove, and the rosy pattern of the old-brick floor, looked cozy and warm. Foster and I were standing in the bluish white snow in front of the window, squinting in the bright sun.

"We could live in it, Mira. Mom is always worried about vandals and everything. We could take care of it for her. And she wouldn't have to pay Mr. Elson to come by twice a week to see that the pipes aren't frozen." It was beginning to sound as though we would be doing Mom a favor.

Mira was looking through the rest of the photo album. She stopped at a picture that Dad had taken on our way to New Milford. I remember the day he took it. It was Christmas, and we were driving up to have Christmas dinner with some friends. As usual, almost as soon as we got on the highway, I had to go. And as usual, Dad got mad. "I told you to go before we left the house," he said.

"I did, but I have to go again."

Every gas station we pulled into was closed. Finally, when we reached Danbury, he stopped on Main Street, and I went into a restaurant that happened to be open. When I came out, Dad was taking pictures of a toy-shop window that had some wind-up toys sitting under a Christmas tree. I remember there was a large one of some beautiful black and white storks, their wings outspread, as they flapped round and round a red brick chimney on a quaint little house. Dad always had a thing for wind-up toys.

I guess I looked so relieved that I finally had found a ladies' room, that he took a picture of me too. That was the one Mira was looking at. In the background you could see the old Danbury *News-Times* building. The one with the dome. It was a white Christmas, and the pavements and streets were covered with snow. All the store windows had tinsely decorations, and cottony fake snow, and lovely big wreaths. It really looked very pretty. But it was the dome on top of the *News-Times* building that Mira was staring at.

"Chtow eto?" she asked. "Roosya?"

"No, not Russia, Mira. America."

"Ameryka," said Mira absolutely wonderstruck. "Ameryka."

"That's in Danbury," I said, as though every other building in the United States had an onion-shaped dome, and the streets were always two feet deep in snow.

"Ameryka," repeated Mira, still staring at the picture. I knew I could get her to go with me then, and that everything was going to be all right.

7

⋯native⋯

The next day was Sunday, so I didn't have school. Israelis work and go to school on Sunday. It's called Yom Rishon, the First Day, and it's the best day in the week for me. I like the feeling of staying home when everyone else is going to school. It's neat having the shops open and going downtown to browse around the bookstores, and having the shopkeepers say, "Lama ot lo ba beit sephir ha yom?" "Why aren't you in school today?"

I went downtown right after breakfast, and went into a travel agency that had posters in the window of skiing in Switzerland. All that snow seemed like a good omen. The girl at the first desk looked nice, so I waited around looking at travel brochures till she wasn't busy.

"Yes?" she asked when I sat down at her desk. "What can I do for you?"

"How much are two tickets to New York?" I had meant to sound matter of fact, as though asking the price of tickets was an everyday thing, but my voice came out all high and quavery.

"Peak season, or off season?" She yawned and looked bored. I didn't know what she meant.

"Both," I answered, figuring that would cover my ignorance.

"Child or adult?"

"One of each."

"Child under twelve?"

"Yes."

"Group flight, forty-five-day excursion, one way?"

That was easy. "One way," I said firmly.

"Tourist, temporary resident, or new settler?"

I was on shaky ground. I knew that I was a tourist, and I thought maybe Mira was a new settler, but I wasn't sure.

"What difference does it make?" I asked.

"Well, a tourist has to pay in foreign currency, like American dollars, or pounds sterling, but a temporary or new settler can pay in Israeli pounds. For a tourist, off season, a child under twelve would pay $293, an adult $556. Peak season is ten percent higher. If you're a temp or new settler, you pay 1,220 Israeli pounds off season for a child, and 2,224.70 for an adult. Ten percent more peak season." She rattled it off so fast, my head was swimming.

"Oh," I said, trying to keep all those numbers from running out of my brain like water through a sieve. "What is it now, peak or off?"

"It will be off season November the fifth. Peak starts

44

again in March. Look, I'll write it all down for you."

When I left the travel agency my legs felt rubbery. I looked at the piece of paper she had given me and tried to figure it out. Right now, all I had was two hundred American dollars and about twenty-five Israeli pounds. As far as I could see, I had no chance of getting the ninety-three extra dollars for my fare. As for the 2,224.70 Israeli pounds for Mira's ticket, forget it.

Still, there must be some way.

I stopped at the nearest shwarma stand, and got a hot shwarma. I wondered how much money Mira could dig up. I knew that the Absorption Agency gave her a monthly allowance, but I was sure she needed it all for food and things. Maybe I could sell something. That little bookstore on Shamai Street bought used books. I bet there were places that bought used clothes and toys. Mira might be willing to sell her samovar and some of her embroidered things. The accordian must be worth a lot. My mind was racing around, and I had a good feeling, as though I could really make it all happen.

I'll say one thing about the Israeli shwarma, and felafel too; they really do put something solid in your stomach that makes you feel as though you could do anything. By the time I was finished eating, I had all kinds of plans in my head. But somehow I was going to have to get Mira to understand that she would maybe have to sell some things, even her accordian. I decided it might be a good idea to bring her some travel folders of the US; some showing snow. I went back to the travel agency. The girl at the desk said, "Oh, you again. Where are you going

45

this time, the French Riviera?"

"I just wanted some travel folders," I said, cool and businesslike.

"Help yourself, they're on the rack." She went back to filing her nails.

I chose some folders of New England. There were pictures of Vermont hills in the winter, little farmhouses looking warm against the blue white snow. There was one of maple-sugaring, the maple trees casting long shadows, and the silvery gray weathered wood of the barn looking so much like home that I could almost smell woodsmoke, feel the pain in my ankles from too much ice skating, and taste the hot chocolate thick with marshmallow when I came up from the pond late on a dark winter afternoon.

On the bus going home, the man sitting next to me asked why I wasn't in school.

"I don't have school today," I answered.

"What school do you go to?" he asked, moving a little closer to me.

"Oh," I said, moving a little bit away, "it's on the Street of the Prophets." He was making me kind of nervous, so I didn't actually tell him the name of the school.

"Excuse me," I said, when we got to my stop. "I get off here."

"I get off here too," he said. He followed me off the bus and caught up with me as I walked down the street past all the bombed-out empty houses.

"Do you have sports in school?" he asked.

"Yes," I answered, walking along as fast as I could.

"Did you have a doctor's examination to see if it's all right for you to take sports?"

"Why do you want to know?" I asked looking sort of sideways at him. He was wearing one of those little skull-caps that means you're religious, but I didn't really like his looks. I mean he looked pretty creepy.

"Well I give that kind of examination," he said. He had a tic in one eye that kept jumping around.

"Are you a doctor?" I asked.

"Not exactly," he answered. "I just give that kind of examination. Why don't I give you one? Then you would know for sure whether it's safe for you to be taking sports in school."

"I think it would look pretty queer to be examined right here in the middle of the street," I answered. And I moved as far away from him as I could, without actually stepping off the curb.

"We could go into one of these empty houses," he said, and the tic in his eye did a regular little dance. We had just come to a corner, and I ducked in back of him and turned real fast, so he was caught walking straight ahead.

"Good-bye," I yelled. "This is where I turn off, and anyway, I had a physical last year so ha-ha!" I ran all the way home looking back every once in a while to make sure he hadn't followed me.

Mom was fixing lunch when I burst in all breathless from having run so fast.

"Describe what he looked like, and I'll call the police," she said, when I finished telling her what had happened. She hacked furiously at the bread she was cutting, her mouth in a grim straight line.

"Well, he was religious, I know that. And he was kind of pale, and sort of old, and he had a pretty active tic."

"That isn't much of a description," Mom said.

"That's all I can tell you about him. Anyhow, I thought you said it was so safe for me here. Like I can go on buses and all and no one will bother me."

"Oh Josie! Let's not go through that again! There are dirty old men everywhere!"

I fingered the travel folders that I had hidden behind my back. Now that Mira and I were going to America, I really didn't have to have that same old argument with Mom anymore. "How come there aren't ever any dirty old women?" I asked.

"That's a very good question," Mom answered, laughing. "A few more like that and you'll qualify as a leader in Women's Lib."

I went over to Mira's right after lunch. As soon as I walked in, I knew something had happened. She had a bright eager look, and her cheeks were more flushed than usual.

"Boodyt moozika," she said, picking up her accordian to show me.

Somehow, I pieced it together that someone from the Ministry of Absorption had come around and asked her to play her accordian in a show with other new immigrants. They wanted her to get integrated into Israeli life, to meet other newcomers, to join an Ulpan—a school especially set up for learning Hebrew. Most newcomers go to an Ulpan, but Mira had never had a chance because of

Mr. Yanovitch's illness. My mother went to one for a while, but she didn't do too well. It makes me grit my teeth to hear her speak Hebrew. But most people in Israel speak English, so she doesn't have to use Hebrew too much anyway.

By the time I had figured out what Mira was trying to tell me, I was too tired to try to explain about the tickets or show her the travel brochures. Let alone try to tell her that going to America would be much better than staying in Israel and going to an Ulpan. Besides, how was I ever going to make her sell her accordian? My head hurt, it was such an effort to think of gestures, bits of Hebrew, English, Russian, anything that I could use to make her understand.

She was smiling happily, and practicing the song that she would sing, so I kissed her on the cheek, and let myself quietly out the door.

Mom woke me up later that afternoon to tell me that Mira was waiting to see me. I hardly ever nap in the afternoon, although most people here do. The stores are all closed from one to four and all the shopkeepers go home to sleep. I got up groggily, my head still aching a little, and went into the kitchen. It is funny to watch Mom trying to talk to Mira. She mostly talks pidgin English very loudly, as though Mira were deaf. Mira looks concerned and serious. Mira had her accordian with her, and when I came into the room, she got up, hoisted the strap over her shoulder and took me by the hand.

"She's going to be in a new-immigrants' show," I said to Mom. "I think she wants me to come with her to the rehearsal."

"That's nice," said Mom, smiling at Mira. She raised

her voice a few decibels. "Be good for you. Meet friends. Start new life." She turned to me. "Be home in time for dinner, Jo-Jo. I'm going out this evening."

The little room the rehearsal was held in was filled with people; Russians, Uzbeks, Rumanians, Iraqis, some with instruments, most without. A small slender man with bushy white hair sat in the corner holding a shopping bag with the head of a perfectly beautiful puppet sticking out of it. Mira spotted him about the same time I did and hurried over to him. They fell into each other's arms and a regular stream of Russian poured out, so fast that I could only catch a few "Ya khachoos" and "Horoshows." Mira was beaming and smiling and wiping the tears from her eyes. The little man had put down his shopping bag, and I slipped my hand in and pulled out the puppet. She was dressed in a gauzy material covered with spangles, and had a fan in her hand. Inside the bag was a fierce-looking king dressed in a robe that had a real fur collar, and a sinister-looking villain all in black. I was just beginning to make the lady puppet fan herself, when a fat man came into the rehearsal room and started to organize things.

It didn't take long to find out that most of the singers should have done their singing in the bathtub. As for the three violinists who scraped out some little tunes, they were strictly for family parties. There was a young man wearing a little Uzbek beanie who played the xylophone, and then there was Mira. She was really the best one. Her voice is sweet, and she didn't put in any of those quavery trills that all the other singers seemed to specialize in.

After Mira had played her piece, Grisha, her friend with the puppets, put on a scene from one of his puppet shows. He knelt behind a chair, using the top of the back as the floor of the stage, manipulating the puppets by their sticks very deftly. The king was madly in love with the lady and wanted to marry her, but then the wicked villain whisked her away. It was lovely.

After that there was a break, and then they did the whole show over again. They were going to do it just like that the following week in front of an audience. The fat man who was acting as master of ceremonies seemed quite satisfied. He gave them some tickets to sell, and sent them home.

Grisha and Mira were yaketing away in Russian, and I knew when I heard him say "chai" that he had invited her to tea. He seemed to be inviting me too, and since I didn't have anything else to do, I sort of tagged along with them. He lived in an Absorption Center in a very poor part of Jerusalem. We had to walk a long way to get to the bus. Mira and I took turns lugging the accordian, while Grisha walked along with quick, rather dainty steps, carrying his shopping bag, the lady puppet's head nodding over the top of it. The people on the bus were crowded together in thick dark hairy lumps, and the smell of garlic wasn't so great either.

When we got off the bus we had to walk again. It was a pretty slummy neighborhood. Clothes strung out on thousands of clotheslines were flapping around in the wind. A regular forest of water tanks and solar heating things and TV antennae was sprouting from the roofs.

The people jammed into those houses must have spent a lot of time doing what my Scripture teacher calls pro-creating because there were kids hanging out of all the windows, and spilling out onto the sidewalks and streets. When we passed, they stopped whatever they were doing to stare. That's the national pastime. Gaping. With your mouth open. Finger exploring your nose.

Grisha and Mira walked ahead of me, not paying any attention to any of them or to me either. Then suddenly, a skinny little kid darted out and kicked me in the shin. Mira turned around so fast, you'd have thought she had eyes in the back of her head. "Tafseek," she yelled, her cheeks getting bright red. After that she held on to my hand, and we walked three abreast down the narrow pavement. When we got to the corner, I looked back, and the little kid was peeing, drawing gigantic circles in the street. He thumbed his nose at me without interrupting his artistic endeavors.

The Absorption Center was the same pale beige stone as all the other buildings in Jerusalem. A sign over the door said "Moadon Rasco." We went up a flight of stairs into a long corridor with lots of doors, some of them open. A few people stuck their heads out and nodded to Grisha. The rooms that I could see into had strange collections of furniture. Mismatched chairs around make-shift tables, old wooden beds covered with tattered cloths, battered cardboard suitcases. And always, shiny brand-new refrigerators and washing machines, the hallmark of the new immigrant taking advantage of his rights.

Grisha's room looked different. He had a tremendous

brass bed that took up most of the room. God knows how he got it here from Russia. It was covered with a magnificent but dirty velvet spread with tarnished gold and silver braiding and glass beads sewn all over it in swirling patterns. Propped all over the bed were puppets, sitting, standing, leaning. Stacks of books took up whatever floor space remained, some of the books still in boxes. One box served as a table, and was covered with a cloth, and set with tea things.

Grisha shared a tiny kitchen with the people who had rooms on either side of his. He made tea, and we sat around the box and drank it. While we were drinking, a very little man looked around the edge of Grisha's door, said something, and disappeared. He came back a minute later with a large plate of herring and hot potatoes and sour cream. A thin young girl came in with a pot full of fish and some plates, followed by a bearded man with a platter of noodles and carrots. They sat down on the floor, or on the bed, and just like that we were having a party! Mira pulled me over close to her, and heaped up a plate of food for me. I had never eaten fish heads before, and wasn't sure I'd like them, or even how to approach them. I watched Verutchka, the thin young girl, sucking noisily on a fish head. The marbelized eye of the fish stared at me until I was forced to look away.

Grisha got a bottle of vodka from under the bed, and some little glasses. Along with the sound of the sucking of fish bones, the smacking of lips over herring, the clink of knives spearing potatoes and carrots, there was the gurgle of vodka being carefully poured into glasses over

and over again. Eating and drinking is serious business
for Russians.

I picked up a fish head gingerly, and tried to bite into
it, but found the only thing to do was suck. It really was
quite good, sweet and very tasty. Mira gave me some
vodka which burnt my tongue. Everybody was talking;
the Russian flowing around and past me. For once, I
didn't feel out of things. Sitting there close to Mira, sucking fish bones and sipping vodka, was the nicest I'd felt in
a long time. After a while, I got a little sleepy, and rested
my head on Mira's shoulder. She moved me gently into
the center of the bed, after shoving some of the puppets
out of the way, and I fell asleep.

It was dark outside when I woke up, and I was scared
to death that Mom would be worried out of her mind. I
remembered seeing a phone in the hall and went out to
call her. I let the phone ring and ring but there was no
answer. "Great," I thought, "she's probably called the
police by now and they're all out searching for me. I'm
really going to get it when I show up."

I went back into Grisha's room. The party was still
going on. "Mira," I said, and tugged her sleeve gently,
"home." She put her finger to her lips. Miron, the tiny
little man, was telling a story and everyone was listening.
There just didn't seem to be any way to get Mira to
leave.

I picked up a puppet and started messing around. It
was a little boy puppet with a big round head and bright
blue eyes. He wore a black wide-brimmed hat and side
curls like a little Chassid, and around his neck he had a

prayer shawl. I held his hands together and made him bob his head up and down as though he were praying, making a low chanting noise at the same time.

"Horoshow," said Grisha. He picked up a large puppet dressed in black, who carried a stick in his hand. The large puppet rapped my little Chassid on the hat with his stick. "Lo tov, lo tov," he said in a deep grumpy voice. My little Chassid put his hands up over his eyes, and I made him cry. Then the big puppet put a tiny open book in the little puppet's hands, and rapped smartly on the book with the stick. "Achad," counted the big puppet in his deep voice, pointing with his stick at a number in the book.

"Achad," I made my little puppet count timorously in a high squeaky voice, pointing his finger at the number.

"Shtayim," counted the big puppet, pointing his stick at the next number.

"Shtayim," counted the little puppet pointing his finger.

"Shalosh," boomed out the deep voice, pointing the stick.

"Arba!" squeaked the little puppet quickly, and thumbed his nose at his teacher. Everybody laughed and clapped their hands.

I looked around embarrassed. I didn't know they had all been watching. I put the little puppet's hands up over his face shyly, and stood there.

Mira hugged me. "Krasavytsa," she said.

"Mira," I said now that I had her attention, "home, HOME. It's late. I've got to get home."

"You are very good with puppets," said Grisha in English. "You will be fine puppeteer someday." He started talking to Mira in Russian, and I could tell he was talking about me.

"Mira," I said getting between her and Grisha, "HOME!" She nodded her head, and went to collect her accordian and purse.

All the way home, I kept thinking of how scared Mom must be. The long walk from the bus was exhausting. Mira and I took turns lugging the accordian up the hill past the convent wall. When we turned the corner into our street, she stopped for a minute to rest and catch her breath. It was terribly late. The moon was hanging very low and large in the sky, almost caught on the point of a delicate tower way over on Mount Scopus. Thousands of little lights glimmered in the tiny Arab houses down in the wadi, and there were lights strung out like beads across the dark dusky hills.

There were no lights on at my house. "Oh God," I thought, "she must be out looking for me." I got Mira to her apartment-house door, and ran across the street, trying to get the keystring off my neck. The house, when I got into it, had that quiet feeling of having been empty for a while. The shutters were still closed against afternoon heat, although it had cooled with the coming of darkness hours ago.

There was a note on the table. "Jo-Jo baby, I've gone to Tel Aviv with Boris. Fix yourself some dinner. There's a can of tuna in the cupboard and some packages of soup. Don't forget to call the wake-up service, and put yourself to bed at a reasonable hour. Love and more love, Mom."

Boris was back, then. Well I didn't care. I wasn't going to mind so much this time. There was always Mira. It didn't really matter that she couldn't understand most of what I tried to tell her. And somehow, I was going to get together enough money so the two of us could go to America. I crumpled the note Mom had left into a ball, and threw it into the garbage. Then I called the wake-up service, washed my face and hands, brushed my teeth, and went to bed.

❧❦❧

9

❧❦❧

$\mathcal{T}$he weeks went slowly by,
and no matter how much I thought about it there just
didn't seem to be any way to raise enough money for
tickets. Things at home started to get really rotten with
Mom being out with Boris again practically every night.
School wasn't much better either. Now that it was winter,
all the girls huddled around the stove during recess, forever whispering. Since the war, we hardly ever had any
heat, and our classroom was dank and gloomy. One day,
Mrs. Farrell decided we needed an outing and announced
that our class was going on a trip to Bethlehem.

"No tatty clothes," she warned. "Everyone is to be suit-
ably dressed." A rickety Arab bus was waiting in the
school compound the next morning.

"Stella, save the seat next to you for me," yelled Maryanne. She was standing in line stamping her feet and rub-

bing her mittened hands while she waited for Mrs. Farrell to check her name off the list.

Fat Rosamunda panted aboard, her breath coming out in steam. I hoped she would sit down next to me so I'd be spared the embarrassment of Mrs. Farrell having to assign a seat partner to me. But she plopped down next to Carlos. "Oh Carlos," she said practically sitting on his lap, "you're taking up too much room." Everyone knows she has a crush on Carlos.

The cute Arab bus driver stopped flirting with Stella and gave Caroline the eye. Caroline stuck her nose up as she sashayed past him wiggling her rear end. Stella glared at her. "Caroline, come sit here," called Jenine El Gazi.

The bus was filling up, and there still was no one in the seat next to me. I wished I'd stayed home with Mira. Mom was going to Haifa with Boris for the day, so she wouldn't have known anyway. I looked out of the window and remembered the day last week when I stayed home with Mira. We'd had such fun! There was beautiful unbelievable snow when I woke up that morning. Snow in Jerusalem! All the olive trees and the pink tile roofs and the little Arab village were covered with a delicate white frosting.

"Mom, Mom," I yelled running barefoot down the icy cold tiled hallway. "There's snow!"

"Josie, get back in bed," she said sleepily from under the piles of blankets, "before you freeze to death."

"Do you think there's school today?" I asked, hopping from one numbed foot to the other.

"Call up and find out," she said, and burrowed further beneath the blankets.

Classes were canceled for the day though there was only about an inch of snow that was already melting in the brilliant sunlight. Mom was fast asleep when I went in to tell her. She'd come in very late the night before, and even the rare sight of snow in Jerusalem was not enough to keep her awake. As soon as I was dressed I ran over to Mira's. Oh, it was gorgeous! There was just enough snow to make a snowlady that we dressed in one of Mira's shawls. Then we had a snowball fight, and Mira's round little cheeks got rosier and rosier. Abu Rauchi laughed when he saw her playing around like a kid.

The snow was all gone by noon, and Mira made hot soup for lunch and tea with spoonfuls of my favorite strawberry preserves. After tea, she brought out a little book, "Moukha Tsokhotoukha." It's a rhyming story about a lady fly who has a birthday party. Every Russian child knows it by heart. Mira taught me how to say it, pointing at each letter and sounding it out, until I knew it by heart, too. I said it now, staring out of the window at the leaves rattling in the trees of the school compound.

"Moukha, Moukha, Tsokhotoukha," I said to myself, sitting there in the bus, "posolochenoyeh brewkho, Moukha po polyou poshla. . . ."

"You have saved this place for me, yes?" Mathias grinned and slid in next to me. I couldn't believe it! I'd rather be the only one on the bus sitting alone than sit with Mathias Glauter! I looked around to see if there were any empty seats. The only one was up front next to Mrs. Farrell, and her shopping bag was sitting squarely in the middle of that.

Mrs. Farrell stood up and clapped her hands for attention. "Now class," she said, "we can all have a most enjoyable trip if we remember to follow certain rules: No standing or walking about while the bus is in motion, and no loud voices. If you wish you may sing hymns very quietly. And while we are in Bethlehem, you are to remember that you represent the Jerusalem Mission School and to act with decorum."

The bus lurched forward and I scrunched myself up as far away as I could from Mathias. Everyone more or less settled down quietly as we headed out of Jerusalem on Derek Hebron. Mathias pulled a little paperback book out of his pocket and held it out to me. "Look," he said flipping the pages. "Is nice book. I show you."

I sort of half looked at the book out of the corner of my eye. It was one of those missionary books for children with games and riddles and comic strips. "Join the dots," it said on one of the pages, "to show Jesus King of the Jews on the cross."

"Here is pencil," said Mathias. "You try, yes?"

"Mathias," I blurted out, "are you trying to convert me?"

"Convert?" he asked looking puzzled. "No, no." He pointed to a comic strip showing the difference between a True Believer and others. "That's mine, you mustn't touch" were the words in the balloon over a little boy's head.

"You can have my share," said the angelic True Believer. There was a prayer underneath the strip: "Lord Jesus, help me to be different, help me not to be selfish, but share all good things you give me. Amen."

Mathias was actually trying to be nice!

I took the pencil and the missionary book, and started to connect the dots on Jesus. Mathias breathed a heavy sigh of approval. Then he reached into his pocket and pulled out a candy bar. "You want?" he asked.

I hesitated a minute. Then I took it. "Thank you," I said as I started to unwrap it. I can't really explain what happened next. All I know is that I took a bite of that candy bar and jumped to my feet gagging and gasping and clutching my throat which felt as though I had swallowed fire and ice at the same time. The partially wrapped candy bar fell to the floor, and Mathias bent to pick it up. I'm not sure if there was a glimmer of an evil smile on his face or not. Certainly whatever expression was on it was wiped out immediately by a look of pain, as still gagging and dancing around, I stomped down heavily on his hand. Just then the bus careened around a curve in the road, and Mathias fell forward and struck his head sharply against the metal rail of the seat in front. A slit opened up in his forehead just like the slot in a piggy bank.

"Yaaa-ow!" he screamed as the blood came pouring out. "She's killed me! Help, help, I'm dying, get me a Band-Aid!"

My voice finally found its way past the burning sensation that had gripped my throat, and I let out a yell that rivaled Mathias's.

"Boys! Girls!" called Mrs. Farrell. "Stop the distur-
bance immediately! What is the meaning of this outrageous behavior?" She came charging down the aisle of
the bus.

"I'm dying, I'm dying," moaned Mathias.

"Now Mathias," said Mrs. Farrell, "do try to be a little
more manly. That's nothing but a scratch." She turned to
me. "Josie," she said severely, "you are not to be trusted
near Mathias. You stay at my side throughout the rest of
the trip." Holding my arm tightly she propelled me to the
front of the bus, removed her shopping bag from the seat,
and pushed me down. Then she got a box of Band-Aids,
a bottle of iodine, and some cotton balls out of her shopping bag, and went to minister to Mathias, who was still
whimpering.

The remainder of the trip I stayed right on top of Mrs.
Farrell, and I got to know quite a bit about her. In fact,
I really got to know more about Mrs. Farrell and her
shopping bag than I did about Bethlehem. I was close at
her side in the echoing transept of the Church of the
Nativity when Rosamunda came up flushed and embarrassed and whispered, "Mrs. Farrell, I just got my period.
What should I do?" Nothing daunted, Mrs. Farrell
reached into her shopping bag and equipped Rosamunda
with a sanitary napkin and two safety pins.

I was trotting along directly behind her down the narrow cobbled lane that leads to the Milk Grotto when
Rajah practically doubled over with the sudden cramps
of shilshul. "Mrs. Farrell, I have to go to a rest room,

please," he said panic stricken. Mrs. Farrell quickly directed him to the Tourist Bureau and her shopping bag provided soothing Sedistal.

I was next to her in the crowded shuk eating humus doused with rancid oil, and watching the Arab bus driver tease Caroline, when Stella, obviously jealous, burst into tears. "Oh, Mrs. Farrell, I have a splitting headache," she complained. "When are we going home?"

Mrs. Farrell asked the bus driver to get a cup of water from one of the stall keepers at the shuk. When he returned, the shopping bag not only supplied an aspirin for Stella but a clean handkerchief as well. Stella managed a weak little smile of thanks, and fluttered her eyelashes at the bus driver as he gave her the water.

I got to thinking about Mrs. Farrell. That kind of well-equipped shopping bag probably goes along with the way she dresses, very prim and old-lady. I bet she isn't any older than Mom. I wondered why she never had children and what Mr. Farrell, who was an observer for the UN was like. She was checking off her list to make sure no one was left behind as we got on the bus for the trip back to Jerusalem. "Josie," she said. "Take the seat in the front next to mine again. Mathias, you sit all the way in the back."

I got on the bus and sat down. Mathias scowled as he passed me.

"You wait," he said, "you just wait."

Maryanne clambered aboard and he moved on. "He sure is nuts about you, you lucky girl." She smiled sympathetically at me.

It was pouring rain when we got to Jerusalem, the sudden, hard-as-nails rain of the Middle East. Our class was dismissed as soon as we arrived. I saw Mrs. Farrell pull a pair of rubbers, a plastic rain hat, and a folding umbrella from her shopping bag. Then I ran for the bus home.

Mira was waiting for me with afternoon tea. She rubbed my hair dry, made me put on her house slippers, and fixed hot tea with strawberry preserves the way I like it. Mom still wasn't back from Haifa, so I stayed and had supper with Mira too.

After supper, Grisha showed up. I hadn't seen him since the new-immigrants show, but he remembered me. "Oh it's the little Chassid," he said when I answered the door. "If I knew you were here I would have brought the puppets. You would like to learn, yes?"

Mira was delighted to see him, and after we had tea again, she brought out her accordian and played for us. We all sang "Ivushka Zelenaya" very softly. It is very wistful and nostalgic sounding. It made me think sadly of Connecticut and how I still couldn't figure out a way to get money for tickets. It must have made Mira sad too, because she got tears in her eyes. Grisha said something to her that made her smile and blink them away. Then I saw the lights go on across the street in our house, so I knew Mom was back. I kissed Mira on the cheek, shook hands with Grisha, and went home.

◈

10

◈

Grisha came almost every day now to the afternoon tea I had with Mira. They had been old friends in Moscow, he told me in his beginner's Hebrew. He hoped to set up a puppet theatre in Israel. But until he learned the language, he was spending his time making new puppets with recognizable Israeli characteristics, like the little Chassid. He had been a professor of puppetry in Russia, teaching everything from how to make puppets to how to teach other people to become teachers of puppetry. He sometimes brought along magnificent books with pictures of unbelievably beautiful puppets. One of the books had pictures of Grisha with some of the puppets he had made. He had really been famous in Russia. He taught me how to use the sticks that manipulate the puppets, and I got quite good at it. We put on shows for Mira, and sometimes she would play the accordian as part of the show.

One afternoon, Grisha told me that he had an idea for putting on a puppet show. He had found a little clubhouse on King George Street behind a vacant lot, that was used as the local hangout for the kids in the neighborhood. It had several rooms, one of them large enough to hold about seventy-five people. He thought it would be a good place to put on a puppet show.

At first, I didn't want to be in it. It was fun putting on shows for Mira, but I wanted to be an actress, and if there was going to be an audience, I wanted them to see me, not the puppet I was working. But then I got to thinking about it.

"Will we sell tickets for the show?" I asked Grisha.

"We will ask the people to leave some money, how much they wish, at the door," he answered.

I tried to figure out how much we might get. If everyone donated a few pounds and there were seventy-five people . . . I got a pencil and paper, but I never had learned to multiply properly. I'd have to ask Maryanne to do it for me. I still had not explained to Mira about going to America. I had shown her the travel brochures, and she loved looking at them. But I didn't know how to begin to tell her that she would have to sell some of her things to get enough money together for tickets. She went to the Ulpan every morning now, and studied her Hebrew at home in the evenings, and although she didn't seem to be learning much, she had settled into the routine and seemed more or less content.

The more I thought about it, the more I liked the idea

of doing the puppet show. Maybe if it worked out we could do more than one and really make some money. And then I would go to that snippy girl in the travel agency and say, "Two tickets to America please, one adult, one child, one way." I could see it in my mind very clearly. She would look surprised, and ask me if I had enough money. I would put it all down on her desk, and wait for her to count it up. Then she would be so polite. She would give me the tickets in their neat little folders, and wish me a pleasant journey. I never got further than that. There were no pictures in my mind for actually getting Mira on the plane, or getting to America, or anything else. But now at least, there did seem to be a possibility of getting some money.

Grisha's idea was simple enough. He had spoken to the custodian of the clubhouse who agreed to let us have the large room on a Saturday night for a share of what we took in.

"We will use only two puppets in the show," said Grisha. "The old teacher and the little Chassid."

"I'll bet the little Chassid always gets the better of his teacher," I said.

"Of course," said Grisha, "and he will sing and dance when he has made the poor old fellow miserable with his tricks."

"And Mira can play the accordian for all his songs and dances!" I hugged Mira. I was really beginning to get excited about the show. "How soon can we do it?" I asked.

"Wait, wait." Grisha held up his hand. "First we

must rehearse till we are perfect. Then also, a show must have an audience. We must let people know about it."

"I could make some posters," I said. "If we put posters in the window of Supersol, people would come."

Grisha thought about it. "It would be better to walk with the posters," he said. "More people would see them that way."

"You mean have a parade?" I asked. "That would be great! We could parade the posters down King George on the Friday before the show. All the kids get out of school early, and everyone is downtown shopping for Shabbat. Hundreds of people will get to see us!"

"It would be good to parade also on Saturday night," said Grisha. "Right before the show."

I made some large posters in Hebrew and English advertising the show. I didn't tell Mom about it. Not the posters, not the show, none of it. It wasn't just that I was afraid she might not let me do it. I was afraid she might start asking questions about what I wanted the money for. Things were pretty bad at home since Boris had gotten back from his European tour. Mom was hardly ever in, dinner was something I threw together for myself, and I don't think she ever bothered to tuck me in anymore. I had checked with her about it, and she looked pretty guilty. Then the week right before the show, we really did have a big fight, or at least, Mom got very mad at me. Actually, I don't think I did anything all that bad.

For some reason, I don't know why, she had decided to doll me up and schlepp me along to one of Boris's concerts. She combed my hair herself, trying to get all the tangles out. "What's the matter, Josie, don't you ever comb your hair?" she asked. "This is a mess."

"Yeah, I comb it. But I never fluff it around that way. What are you trying to do, make me look even more like a baby?"

"Hold still," she yanked my head. "You've got a rat's nest here that I can't get out."

"Ow! That hurts! I bet you just want to impress Boris. You want him to think you're such a great mother!"

"Be quiet and put this on." She pulled a little French blue dress, dotted all over with tiny strawberries, and a white pinafore out of my closet.

"I'm not wearing that! You just want me to look baby-ish so everyone will think you're younger than you are! The sweet young mother with her sweet little daughter. Forget it!"

"Josie, I don't want to argue about this. Now hurry up. We're going to be late."

When we got to the concert, which was at some music center way up in Ein Kerem, she fluttered around saying hello to everyone she knew and introducing me. They all oohed and aahed, and said "Hamuda!" "How sweet!" or "Nechmada." I really felt like a first-class idiot.

Then we all went into the auditorium, which wasn't much larger than our living room at home, although it had a tiny stage up front. Mom sat in the front row with her friends, but I didn't like the idea of being her prize exhibit, so I sat a few rows behind her. We sat through a long and boring piece, with Boris thumping away on the piano as though he meant to show it who was boss. I think he made his point, because everyone clapped and yelled bravo when he finished, and he bowed and smiled and looked smugger than usual.

During the interval was when I first got into trouble. They were serving cookies and drinks downstairs in the lounge, and I helped myself and sat down to sample as many of the different varieties as I could lay my hands on before they were all gobbled up. A tall blond bearded guy sat down next to me. He was wearing a dark green velvet suit which right away made me jumpy. When Dad was around, he sometimes brought home producers and people like that from the ad agency. I never could stand the kind that made you feel as though it was a suit wearing a man instead of the other way around. This bearded guy said to me, "Are you enjoying the concert?" I mumbled something with my mouth full of cookie, which I thought sounded more or less polite. But that wasn't enough for him. "What do you want to do when you grow up?" he asked, in that special voice that some grown-ups reserve for children. The kind that lets you know right away that this guy thinks he's great with kids. I swallowed my cookie, took a sip of juice, and said, "I'm going to be an actress."

"Oh," he said, "that's very interesting." He had a British accent and I really hated the way he talked to me, as though I should be flattered by his attention. I was about to stand up and leave, when he said, "I'm in that line of work too. I'm a movie director. Perhaps when you're grown up, and an actress, I'll ask you to be in one of my movies."

72

I let that sink in a minute. Then I turned to him and said coolly, "Sir, perhaps it might be the other way around. Perhaps when I'm grown up, and an actress, I might ask you to be my director." And I got up and walked away. It turned out he was a friend of Boris's. He told Mom about our conversation before the interval was over. I could see them both laughing about it, but she looked at me where I was standing at the table picking over a few broken cookies that had been left, and her eyes were shooting bullets at me.

"How could you be so rude!" she said through clenched teeth as we went up for the second half of the concert. She held my hand and nodded and smiled very sweetly to everyone, but she was digging her nails into my palm. "He's a friend of Boris's; one who can help him a lot. There's no reason to be so snotty."

For the first time, I got the feeling that Mom didn't belong here. That she should go back to America. She never used to worry about being nice to people just because they could help her career. Back home, her friends had been her friends, period. Not useful people. "Boy," I thought, "if only you could hear yourself. You'd be so ashamed, instead of angry at me."

Boris must have knocked the piano temporarily out of service, because when we got back to the auditorium they had put a harpsichord in its place. He came out on the stage, bowed and smiled, lifted his tails, and slid his fat ass onto the piano bench. I guess that's one of the things that bothers me about him. I don't like men with fat asses. There's a lovely word for it: steatopygous. I read that some place. When I was little, one of my favorite dolls was definitely steatopygic. Her name was Poor Pitiful Pearl.

I like the way the harpsichord sounds. Boris played a couple of pieces, getting up between each of them, leaving the stage after all the clapping, and coming back again. Then he played something I really liked. It was by Bach, the *Capriccio for the Departure of My Beloved Brother*. During the Lament, all those cookies and drinks that I had had during the interval got to me, and though I tried to repress it, I belched rather loudly. The combination of belching and Bach made me remember the game I used to play with Dad.

He and I have one thing in common: We can belch at will. We used to have belching tournaments. "VI VAL DI!" he would belch very loudly.

"CO REL LI!" I would answer, topping him.

"SCAR LAT TI!" he'd burp up.

"PA GA NI NI!" I'd belch, and so on. We always belched composers' names, especially those Italians. They make great resonant belches.

Before I knew it, and forgetting where I was, I had come out with a really marvelous ROS SI NI, followed by PUC CI NI, VER DI, and I was going straight on through all of Italian opera, very much in command of all the nuances of each glorious reverberation, when I noticed a deathly silence.

Boris had stopped playing, and everyone had turned around and was staring at me. Here and there, a few people managed a "sshh" or two, but generally everyone must have been too overwhelmed by those really masterful belches to do anything but stare. Then, down in the front row, I saw Mom, her face pale and controlled, but her eyes murderous.

Now that it was quiet, Boris resumed his playing, without even a glance in my direction, and everyone settled down and forgot all about me. Everyone except Mom. She just about had hysterics when she got me out of there. All the way home in the car, she screamed at me. I couldn't help thinking though, Dad would have been proud of me.

❦

11

❦

$\mathcal{M}$om was mad at me all the rest of the week. Not really mean mad, but not exactly her soft, preoccupied-with-more-important-matters attitude toward me, either.

"Josie," she said to me the next evening at dinner. She was home for a change. Boris had gone to play at a kibbutz up in the Galilee, and she hadn't wanted to go. "Why are you being so hostile to Boris? Or to any man in my life, for that matter," she added. "Why can't you accept the fact that I am going to have a life that involves more than my being your mother? Mothers do have lives apart from their children, you know."

"I can accept that. I just can't accept the fact that I had to be dragged off to this dismal place, away from everything I love."

"I don't see how you can call this a dismal place," she

said sharply. "It's one of the most beautiful cities I've ever been in. And most of the people here are as warm and kind as anyone you ever knew at home. More maybe, because of that special feeling of kinship. How can you say that the little Wasp town we lived in is everything you love?"

I didn't answer, just sat there, dipping a piece of pita into khatzilim. I knew part of what she said was true. I remembered the time I had gone shopping downtown on Ben Yehuda Street. After getting some pencils, a large box of Caran D'Ache, and some Bazooka bubble gum, I went to the bus stop. I lined up in the queue, and waited among the usual assorted pushy types. When the bus came, I was more or less carried up the steps by the suitcase of a large man in back of me. I turned and gave him a dirty look, which he returned with interest.

"Fare please, fare," said the driver irritably. He was a square-faced, blue-eyed, no-nonsense sabra, the blond hair on his head as frizzy as the hair on the thick pink thighs that bulged from his khaki shorts.

"Move to one side, please," he said as I started to fumble around in my purse.

I thought I had enough money to get home, but there wasn't a solitary agora left in my purse. "I can't find my money," I said.

"You'll have to find another way home then," said the driver briskly, and opened the door.

Almost immediately, half the pushy shovey types on the bus were pushing and shoving their way up to the front with bus fare for me in their outstretched hands. The large man with the suitcase fell over it in an attempt to pay my fare. I knew that their eagerness to help did have to do with that special feeling Mom was always talking about. Just as I knew when I sat down that the lady next to me was genuinely interested in helping me read the Hebrew on my Bazooka comic. And that she was genuinely pleased when I told her that I could read the Hebrew on my own. But that didn't change my feelings any.

"Look," I said to Mom. "What difference do you think it makes to me that all of Israel thinks they're my family? I don't especially want them to be my family. They always have to be better than everyone else, and smarter. And besides, most of them are terribly rude."

"Listen, my little Jewish American Princess. You expect people who were packed into sealed boxcars and sent to concentration camps, people who right now, every single day of their lives, are threatened with total destruction to have the social graces of a debutante?"

"Well, I don't see why so many of them have to act as though they never heard of a handkerchief."

"Josie, honestly, you just sound silly! Do you think all those rough tough pioneers that opened up the American West used handkerchiefs? This is a pioneer country, and lots of the pioneers here come from places where they never even heard of running water, let alone handkerchiefs. The miracle is not that this crazy pressure-pot mix of nationalities with nothing in common but their need for a homeland is making the desert bloom. The miracle is that they are doing it with such apparent ease that twerps like you can criticize and be hostile because they're not your A.O.K. regulation American suburban kind of polite!"

"I still don't like it here," I said. "I don't like the school I go to. I don't have any friends. I stay at home by myself most of the time. Maybe it's not that I'm hostile, it's that I'm unhappy."

I could tell she was upset when I suggested that perhaps she went out too often because she got that strained look around her mouth. "I don't think you are being entirely truthful," she snapped. "I think you are very hostile. You are angry at me most of the time. What makes you think you'll be happier in any other school with any other kids? It's still going to be you, no matter where you are."

"Are you saying there's something wrong with me?" I asked. "That I'll never be happy, never have friends?" I was practically shouting.

"See, that's what I mean. There it is, all that hostility directed at me."

"I'm not directing hostility at you. I just can't make you understand what it's like for me here, that's all."

We did the washing up without saying much to each other. Then I went out on the balcony to do my homework. Mom followed me out after a while, holding a skein of yarn.

"Josie," she said, "will you hold this for me while I wind?" She was knitting a sweater for Boris, a beautiful soft blue gray.

"If there is any wool left over can I have it?" I asked, holding my arms in place for the yarn. I was thinking of how cute a little puppet would look dressed in a blue gray sweater. She didn't answer, but looked across the street. Grisha was just rounding the corner on his way to Mira's house. He waved when he saw us.

"Do you know him?" Mom asked.

"Yep, that's Grisha. He's a friend of Mira's." I was going to add "and mine" when Mom interrupted.

"I didn't know Mira had a beau," she said, surprised. "That's nice for her, isn't it?"

"He's not her beau." I dropped my arms, and the wool tangled. "He's just a friend. He's my friend too. I can make friends, you know."

"Josie, lift up your arms, the wool is getting tangled. And don't put words in my mouth. I didn't say you can't make friends. What I said was that you were hostile to me most of the time."

"Let's not do that whole thing again," I answered. We finished the wool in silence, but the hard tight feeling that I had in my stomach didn't go away till I went across to Mira's.

She greeted me at the door as usual, her face rosy and welcoming. We hugged each other, and went into the kitchen where Grisha was already drinking tea.

"Oh, here is the little Chassid," he said. "Come sit down and have some tea. Then we must work."

We practiced almost every evening now as well as afternoons, going over and over the little skit Grisha had written. He was still adding bits of new material, trying to perfect it for the performance, which was scheduled for that Saturday night. Mira poured my tea, and sat down close to me.

"Was that your mother?" Grisha asked. "I would like to meet her. I would like to tell her what a talented little Chassid you are. But of course she will see for herself on Saturday."

"Not on your life she won't." The words were startled out of my mouth before I knew it.

"What did you say?" Grisha asked, puzzled.

"It's just an Americanism," I lied. But I was a little shook at the idea of Mom showing up at the puppet show. It had never occurred to me before, and it didn't fit in with my plans at all.

More and more I planned and thought of going home. I dreamt asleep and awake of being back in Connecticut. Always in my waking dreams, Mira was there. Sometimes I pictured her sitting in our kitchen, waiting for me when I came running up the driveway after school. Sometimes we were walking in the woods together on a snowy day, her cheeks like little red apples from the cold. Sometimes we would be sitting in front of our fireplace and Mira would be playing the accordian softly and singing a Russian song, the firelight flickering on her dear face. I moved closer to her as I finished my tea, and she leaned over and kissed me gently on the top of my head.

"Your mother will be very proud of you." Grisha interrupted my thoughts.

"Yes, yes she will," I answered. Mom would be proud. She admired any kind of talent, and according to Grisha, I was talented. Mom had made a great fuss over me the night I played Potiphar's wife. Well, too bad. There was no way I was going to tell her about Saturday night.

❦

12

❦

The only subject I could get even mildly interested in at school that week was Math. One day during recess I tried to get Maryanne to work out how much I might earn at the show if a possible seventy-five people showed up and each of them donated anywhere from one to ten pounds.

"That is," I told her, "you have to consider that it will be divided three ways, and a percentage taken off for a fourth party."

"What's all this about?" she asked, frowning. "I don't remember this problem as part of our assignment."

"It isn't really," I said evasively. "It's just a friend of mine is going into business and . . . ."

"Maryanne," Rosamunda called from the other end of the yard where a group of girls were playing Seven Up. "Bring over your Goomie. No one wants to play this stupid game anymore." Rosamunda spends most of every recess eating. She comes from a roly-poly English family. Her mother is roly-poly, her father is roly-poly, and the baby I see propped up in the car when they come to pick her up is roly-poly. Her father is a newspaper correspondent. Every time he comes back from the home office in London he brings stocks of Marmite and plum pudding and Cheshire cheese. Rosamunda tells us about them, her eyes glistening. She can make Marmite sound like a Baskin-Robbins mandarin chocolate ice-cream cone. Today her mother, just to make sure that Rosamunda didn't starve between breakfast and lunch, had provided her with several pitas spread thick with black gooky Marmite paste. "Come on, Maryanne," she called, her mouth stuffed. "We're waiting."

"I'll work this out later, Josie luv," said Maryanne getting up from the pile of rocks we were sitting on. She took her Goomie out of her pocket, and went over to join the group. I looked at the numbers Maryanne had written on the piece of paper.

"Is love letter?" Mathias sidled up to me and tried to look over my shoulder.

"Oh Mathias, mind your own business," I said, and then I wished I hadn't. His face got even meaner and nastier than usual.

"Is love letter," he said twisting my arm. "Give."

"Oh for Christ's sake, Mathias, stop being an idiot."

"You take the name of our Lord in vain." He twisted my arm even harder.

"Quit it, you're hurting me." I tried to pull my arm away.

"Mathias, let go of Josie." It was Catherine who had stopped playing Goomie and come over into the shade. "Leave her alone, or I'll tell my father."

"I tell him she blasphemes our Lord," said Mathias, but he dropped my arm.

"Gawd, am I ever hot." Maryanne, her face beaded with sweat, plunked herself down on the pile of rocks. "Is Mathias at it again?" she asked. "You really ought to tell your Mum. I think it's dreadful what he does to you."

"I've told my mother. She thinks I'm making it up."

"Well, you bring her around here. I'd tell her so she'd believe me."

The bell rang, and we walked slowly into the long shadowy school corridor. The pale pink uneven blocks of the old stone floor shone dimly beneath the light filtering in through the tree-shaded windows. Maryanne had her arm around my waist. It was one of those days when her best friend Stella was absent.

"Let's sit together at lunch," she said. She squeezed my hand as we walked into Mr. Vandervoss's class.

Mathias turned around when we came in and gave me a nasty look. "I fix you good." I could read his lips as he silently mouthed the words. I slid into my seat and looked the other way. I knew he meant to get me into trouble because Catherine stuck up for me. There was really nothing I could do about him. I thought of talking about it to Maryanne. But at lunch she sat with Rajah, and when I went over to join them, she didn't pay any attention to me at all.

Maryanne is really the only girl at school I'd like to be

friends with. Mostly because she is nice and very kind, which is more than I can say for fat Rosamunda. But she never invites me to go to the movies with her, or to her house after school, or anything like that. Of course, she has Stella, and they don't need anyone else.

After school, I went to Mr. Vandervoss for extra help. "Mr. Vandervoss," I said, moving out of range of his breath, "I'm having such a hard time with percentages. Could you please go over the lesson with me?" Actually, I hoped to work him around to the problem that Maryanne hadn't finished.

He looked over his glasses at me. He was about to leave, his books under his arm, his string shopping bag in hand, ready for his daily trip to Supersol. I see him there every once in a while, but I always make a point of avoiding an encounter with him. It would be too embarrassing to have him know that I'm aware of his pitiful little expenditures. He always buys the same things: one yogurt, one tomato, one bagel, one pint of milk.

"Vell, Joosie. This is a pleasant surprise that you are now interested in improvement." He put his string bag and his books down on the desk, and picked up a piece of chalk. "Come, I show you."

He had just gone to the board, and was starting to write a series of numbers, when there was a dreadful screaming in the hall and the sound of footsteps running toward us. Mrs. Farrell burst into the room. "Dirk, Dirk, come quickly," she said to Mr. Vandervoss. "Mathias has had some sort of fit. He's fainted dead away."

They both ran out of the room, and I followed as far

as the doorway. There, sure enough, on the floor of the hallway, was Mathias. A few scared-looking kids were standing around and staring down at him.

"All right, boys and girls," said Mrs. Farrell. "Don't stand about gaping. Hurry along home now." She started fanning Mathias briskly with a palm-leaf fan that she took out of her shopping bag. Her stringy legs were exposed right up to her thighs as she bent over Mathias with her sensible skirt hitched up, fanning him energetically.

"It might help if we sponged his forehead with a damp cloth," she said to Mr. Vandervoss.

Mr. Vandervoss sprinted down to the men's room and came back with a cup of water which he threw on Mathias's face. Mathias moaned and stirred a bit.

"He's coming to," said Mrs. Farrell. "I wonder if you'd be able to get him home, Dirk. He lives out in Beit Jallah. No use trying to ring up his parents. They've no phone. You'd better take a taxi. Sorry to leave you with this, but I've got an appointment." And she got up, pulled her skirt down, put the fan back into her shopping bag, patted her hair, and trotted off on her long thin legs as though the whole thing were no concern of hers.

Mr. Vandervoss looked around the empty hallway as though he expected help to come from somewhere. Then he sighed and leaned over Mathias. "Mathias, Mathias, I take you home now. You stand up, yes? I help you."

Mathias moaned, and stirred some more. I don't know why, but standing there behind the door, I suddenly got the feeling that Mathias was putting on an act. There was just something so fake about the way he was fluttering his eyelids, and letting little helpless sounds escape through his lips. I could do a lot better if I had his part. He pulled himself slowly up until he was resting shakily on one elbow, and looked around, possibly to see how large an audience he had. I guess he was disappointed, because he let out a really heartrending moan, and flopped down on his back again.

"Mathias, come, I help you." Mr. Vandervoss pulled Mathias up to a sitting position. "You sit here and await me, yes?" Mr. Vandervoss patted Mathias encouragingly on the back, heaved a sigh of relief, and came back to the Math room to get his string bag and books.

He seemed startled to see me waiting there. "We cannot work longer today," he said hurriedly gathering his things. "We work tomorrow again, yes?" I nodded my head in agreement and he left the room.

I watched him help Mathias to his feet and escort him down the corridor and through the front door. I waited until I could no longer hear the crunch of their feet on the gravel path, and then I got my things and left the school. Mr. Vandervoss and Mathias were nowhere in sight when I came out through the green iron gates onto the street. They must have gotten a cab immediately.

Mr. Vandervoss didn't keep his promise about helping me after school the next day, or the day after that either, because he didn't come to school. I guess he found the trip out to Beit Jallah too exhausting. Mathias didn't come to school again for the rest of that week either, but that didn't exactly make me beat my breast or rend my clothes.

⋘⧫⧫⧫⋙

13

⋘⧫⧫⧫⋙

All of Jerusalem must have
been on King George Street that Friday at noon. Grisha
and Mira and I stumbled off the bus above Independence
Park near Terra Sancta ready for our parade. Grisha was
carrying the posters, which were attached to long sticks
that had goosed any number of passengers and now got
stuck in the rear door as we disembarked.

"Tiftach! Tiftach!" yelled Mira, her face red as she
pounded on the door. Several bystanders moved a little
closer making an instant crowd. The little Arab newsvendor, who had been chanting, *"Ma'ariv, Yediot, Post,
Post,"* now started yelling, *"Tiftach et ha delet,"* along
with Mira, and crossing his eyes seductively at me.

At school that morning, I had begun to worry that I'd
be recognized by some of the kids from my class while
I paraded. So I stopped off at home and borrowed quite

a bit of Mom's expensive American makeup, hoping she wouldn't notice when she got back from Shabbat shopping. I put on base, eye shadow, mascara, blusher, lip gloss, the works. Actually my face felt stiff under all that gook, but I did look different.

Mira held up both hands and said, "Ma kara?" when she saw me, and several ladies on the bus said, "Ma pitome! Ze lo Purim!" But it apparently excited the little Arab newsvendor beyond all endurance. He skipped around and grinned at me, puckering up his mouth and making little kissing noises, and crossed his eyes repeatedly, while I tried to look cool and oblivious. Finally, the bus driver opened the door, Grisha pulled the posters free, the crowd dispersed, and we crossed to the shady side of the street.

Once there, we started our parade. Grisha gave me one of the posters and I held the stick in my left hand so the message I had lettered in Hebrew and English was lifted above my head:

COME SEE! COME SEE!
SINGING DANCING PUPPETS!
A SHOW FOR YOUNG AND OLD!

Tucked under my arm was one of those little clay drums from the Old City, its goatskin head in the proper position for my free right hand to beat on it. My rhythm was a bit tentative at first, but gradually it assumed a distinctive beat: Thwock, da boomdiddy boom. Thwock, da boomdiddy boom. Mira came a few paces behind me, playing a sort of Slavic march on her accordian. Grisha walked behind her, intoning in his high-pitched voice, "SATURDAY NIGHT, EIGHT O'CLOCK, AT THE YOUTH CLUB!" while the poster he held aloft screamed in Day-Glo paint:

COME SEE! COME SEE!
PUPPETS!

Almost immediately, a few schoolchildren, their schoolbags flapping on their backs, started trotting along with us.

"Ma ot ossa, ma ot ossa?" they yelled, as they crisscrossed back and forth in front of me. "Why are you all painted up, are you one of the puppets?" one of them asked, sticking his face up close to mine. He was eating a shwarma, and bits of meat spewed out of his mouth onto my hair. I felt safe enough behind the mask of all that makeup to say, "You better get out of here, you little bastard, or I'll get my father to beat the shit out of you!"

He looked back at Grisha. "Ha! He looks like a puppet too. He couldn't even hurt me." But he moved back and got lost in the crowd.

Everyone hurries Friday noon in Jerusalem. There is all the marketing to be done before the stores close, the buses stop running, and Jerusalem settles into a tranquil pre-mechanized hush. Our little parade made quite a stir in the crowds elbowing their way down King George intent on their Friday chores. Everyone stopped and stared: women, their shopping bags heavy with chalas, eggplants, avocados, chicken for Shabbat chicken soup; men in business suits or khaki shorts carrying briefcases and bunches of Shabbat flowers; vendors hawking prachim and bagels. It was very satisfying.

We paraded down the length of King George to Rehov Strauss, where the crowds started to thin out. Then we turned up Jaffa and gave those people a treat. About halfway up to Kikar Zion, Grisha's voice gave out, and we stopped at a juice stand to get something to drink. We leaned our posters up against the wall, their messages turned inward. Mira unstrapped her accordian and wiped her face with a large bandanna. I put my drum down and flexed my arm which was cramped from being in the same position for so long. The few remaining schoolchildren who had accompanied us down Rehov Strauss dispersed.

I watched the stream of juice pouring into the glass, and was so thirsty I forgot to think about how the glass went unwashed from one customer to the next. Suddenly, I heard a clinking on the sidewalk. A tourist, coming out of the American bank next door, had thrown a few coins into my drum which was resting open end up on the sidewalk. Some of the coins had missed their mark and landed on the pavement. A woman, passing with a little girl, gave her a ten agorot piece. She toddled over and threw it into the drum, sucking her thumb all the while. A few seconds later, a bearded old man hurried past, murmured, "Miskenim," and threw a coin into the drum. Now that our posters were out of sight, Mira holding her accordian, and I with my painted face, had been mistaken for beggars. The kind that sing and dance and hold out a hat, or in our case, my drum.

The coins were clinking in at a steady rate. Mira, obviously quite upset, said something to Grisha, who was paying for the drinks and hadn't noticed our new profession. On the other side of the American bank, a bona fide beggar, his leprous leg thrust out for all to see, raised a clenched fist at us and started shouting in a hoarse voice. Immediately a crowd collected and sides were taken.

"He's right, he's right, this is his spot; he's been here for years," shouted one man.

"What kind of right? Did he pay key money? This is a free country!" answered another.

"Ha! Some free country. In this country you need *protectsia* even to be a beggar."

"We wouldn't have so many beggars if the government didn't give new immigrants all those rights."

"So, without new immigrants we wouldn't have a country. Maybe your father or your father's father wasn't an immigrant?"

"Sure, but he didn't need rights like washing machines and refrigerators. He was an idealist. The only right he needed was to clear the swamps and get malaria."

"You want to tell me your father is better than mine?" They were almost ready to come to blows, having forgotten all about the original issue. Even the leprous beggar had stopped his hoarse protests against us and was taking sides in the new fight.

Grisha, holding on to the upside-down posters, grabbed Mira by the arm. Mira took me by the hand, and we

started to push our way through the crowd as unobtru-
sively as possible. At the outer edge of my vision, I was
aware of an unpleasantly familiar something. I turned my
head to look, and was not sure, as the crowd shifted and
blotted out his face, whether I had seen or imagined
Mathias.

~§~

14

~§~

$\mathcal{M}$om left early Saturday morning for Tel Aviv with Boris, leaving me free for the day.

"He's doing a concert at the museum," she said coldly, "and considering the way you acted at Ein Kerem, you better not come along." She was carefully applying lipstick with her little brush, tilting her head back to get a more flattering view of herself in the mirror.

"All you care about is Boris," I said. But at the same time I was glad she would be out of the way. She didn't answer, but looked at the pot of lipstick.

"Josie, have you been at my makeup? This is half used up. And my eyeliner looks like someone's been at it. I'll fire Aida if she's been using my things." She swept past me, the hem of her long Arab dress trailing over my bare toes, and picked up a bottle from the dresser. "At least she hasn't used my perfume." She sprayed her throat and behind her ears. "This stuff is impossible to get here."

The doorbell rang. "Josie, will you run and open the door, it must be Boris." There was a panting and scrabbling at the door, and when I opened it, Khumie, Boris's spoiled brat of a dog, dashed in, pulling Boris on the leash behind him.

"You're not taking Khumie to the concert, are you?" Mom asked, giving her cheek to Boris to kiss.

"No, I'm dropping him off at my mother's in Talbieh for the day. He hates to be alone." Boris is crazy about that dog, and has made a big fat oaf of him.

"Maybe he could stay here with Josie," Mom said, pushing Khumie's nose out from between her legs, which was always the first place he went for.

I love dogs, but I really hate Khumie. Whenever he comes to the house with Boris he manages to ruin something of mine. Last time it was the two smallest dolls that are part of a set of nested dolls Mira gave me. They were my favorites, too. Now when I open the big doll, I always know that the tiniest one will be gone, and the next to the tiniest all dogtoothed.

"I think Khumie will be happier with my mother," said Boris, a little stiffly. Apparently he hadn't forgiven me for Ein Kerem either. I gave him the finger behind his back and said, "I can't take care of him anyway. I'm going to spend the day with Mira."

"You'll be all right, won't you, sweetie?" Mom bent to kiss me, enveloping me with the familiar smell of her perfume, all fruity like nectarines and raspberries in the warm sunlight. "There's leftover cholant in the refrigerator, and lots of salad stuff. Invite Mira over here to eat. You can stay up and watch TV if you want to, but put yourself to bed by eleven thirty. I'll be home very late."

They breezed out the door, Khumie straining at the leash, the sound of his nails on the marble steps like the sound of chalk on blackboard.

I looked out the window to make sure they were gone before I went over to Mira's. Boris was holding the car door open for Mom. She lifted her long skirt gracefully, got in, and looked up at him, smiling. I wonder if Boris thinks Mom is sexy. She has beautiful clothes. Long gauzy skirts, little clingy tops that she doesn't wear a bra under, embroidered Arab dresses, shawls with fringes, a deep-violet cape. She's promised to give them all to me when I'm grown up.

All of a sudden I thought of the psychiatrist I had gone to before we came to Israel, Dr. Mouldy. "Tell me about your mother's lovers," he said the first time I saw him. "Does it bother you that she sleeps with men?"

"I don't think she'd like me to discuss it," I answered. The creep. If he wanted a cheap thrill why didn't he go to an X-rated movie.

They drove off, the car raising a spray of gritty white sand behind it, and I went over to Mira's. Abu Rauchi salaamed, "Keef haleck," as I crossed the street. The words rose slowly into the bright white heat haze.

We spent most of the day rehearsing for the puppet show that evening. Grisha and I went over and over our parts, and Mira played the accordian for us whenever it was needed. In between songs, she acted out the part of the audience, clapping and laughing when the little Chassid outsmarted his teacher, hissing and booing when the teacher was mean.

We stopped at about two thirty, and I helped Mira get Shabbat lunch. I spread a clean white tablecloth on the kitchen table, and set it while Mira heated up a pot of thick borscht. She had made sweet and sour cabbage rolls, chicken and mashed potatoes. I ran home to get the cholant Mom had left, and while that was heating made a salad of tomatoes, avocados, and cucumbers, all chopped up, Israeli style. Mira clucked around me like a mother hen, and acted as though my salad were a minor miracle.

After lunch, she made me lie down for a while, making sure the trissim were open to let in the cool air. I must have fallen asleep because the next thing I knew, the piece of sky I could see from the couch was a pale lavender with drifts of amber clouds, and the air was quickening with the feeling of Jerusalem stirring to life as Shabbat ended. The bells of the convent were tolling the nuns to evening prayer. They always seem louder on Shabbat because everything else is so hushed and dreamy. The nuns are of the Order of Saint Clare and have taken a vow of silence; the bells do all the talking for them. Sometimes I go up on our roof and look down into the walled convent garden. You can see the nuns in their wide-brimmed gardening hats, the blue skirts of their habits tucked up into their aprons, working in long neat peaceful rows among the olive trees and vegetables.

I lay there for a while listening to the bells, not quite

wanting to get up yet. Mira and Grisha were having tea in the kitchen, and she poured me a cup when I came in yawning and rubbing my eyes.

"Ot otzbanite?" asked Grisha. "Are you nervous?"

"No," I answered. But I took my cup and snuggled up close to Mira.

We collected our posters and puppets and as soon as the buses were running again we took one to King George, and walked over to the Youth Club. The custodian was waiting for us at the door. He had arranged folding chairs in the large main room facing a small puppet theatre that Grisha had constructed. Mira and I were delighted when we saw the puppet theatre. It was very simple, made of heavy cardboard glued to strips of wood; three sections hinged together like a folding screen.

"Hamuda, hamuda," said Mira smiling happily. She lifted up the crepe-paper curtain that covered the window in the center section. I stood in back of the window, which was just high enough for me to manipulate my little Chassid without being seen, and bowed him right and left. Grisha fussed around with the folding chairs, while the custodian set up a table near the door with a large copper kettle on it. At first the custodian wanted to pass the kettle around before the show started.

"It will be very good to have Mira play something lively while I offer everyone the possibility of contributing something for the sake of the artists," he said. He put a few coins in the kettle and shook it so that they clinked suggestively.

"No, no, no," said Grisha. "Ze lo naim. It's not nice.

Also people give more if they have already enjoyed the show."

"O.K., O.K., you're the boss," said the custodian. He set the kettle on the table so that people could put something in it on the way out.

By now it was seven thirty, and we left the puppets in the clubhouse and went out with our posters for a pre-show parade.

The streets were thronged with Saturday-night revelers. Up and down Shamai and Ben Yehuda and on King George down to Jaffa it was so crowded that it was hard to walk. After a long day of enforced quiet, the chach-chachim, the whores, and the teenagers were ready for anything. They swarmed over the streets bringing car and bus traffic almost to a standstill. Our little parade could hardly be seen, and after a short time we managed to fight our way back to the clubhouse.

≈§≈

15

≈§≈

When we got back, the hall
was filling up. The custodian scurried around setting up
extra folding chairs as more and more people wandered
in. Standing on tiptoe behind the puppet theatre, Mira
and I could peek out and watch without being seen. At
first, I counted heads. But when I got to fifty, I found myself counting the same head twice as people milled about,
so I stopped counting and just watched.

Mira squealed happily and pinched me as a large group
of her classmates from the Ulpan filed in. "Ot ro'a! Ot
ro'a!" she said to me, pointing them out.

Some of the kids who used the other rooms in the clubhouse came in, along with a contingent of Grisha's friends
from Moadon Rasco. I recognized Miron and Verutchka
who were heading up a large party of other Russian immigrants. There were quite a few of the American pen-

sioners that I see whenever I shop at Supersol. You can always spot them because their shopping carts are filled with expensive imports like Heinz baked beans and Maxwell House coffee.

I saw a few faces that looked like some of the people who had stared at our parade on Friday. The schoolboy who had pushed up against me was there, along with his mother and father and a swarm of younger children. They croaked gutturally at one another as they played some form of Sephardic musical chairs with the littlest one ending up on the floor crying.

"Your mother, she's not coming?" asked Grisha looking out at the crowd. "I do not see her." He turned to me, alarmed. "You gave her properly the address?"

"She couldn't come," I answered. "Her best friend is very sick, practically on her deathbed. Mom has to stay with her and feed her intravenously."

Mira's eyes widened sympathetically when Grisha translated for her, and she reached over and patted me on the cheek so lovingly that I felt momentarily guilty. But only momentarily. I was getting more and more excited as the crowd got bigger and bigger. My hands were clammy with sweat, but I wasn't a bit nervous. When the hall was filled to capacity and the custodian had brought in the last of the folding chairs, he closed the door.

"Break a leg," Grisha whispered to me in true theatrical tradition. Then he stepped out in front of the puppet theatre and bowed.

"You are about to see," he told the audience in his halting Hebrew, "an original puppet show, written and directed by one of the world's leading puppeteers. I have come from Moscow after a long struggle, a trial by fire, to the beloved and longed-for homeland, Eretz Israel. This show is a greeting to my new country, and my thanks."

He had the crowd in the palm of his hand; there probably wasn't a dry eye in the place. And when Mira stepped out and played a group of Israeli songs, Yerushalayim shel Zahav, Hevaynu Shalom Alechem, Hava Negila, and ended up with Hatikva, we could have done anything and they would have loved us. There was a general cheering and stamping and whistling. When the crowd quieted down, Mira lifted the crepe-paper curtain and the little Chassid was discovered sitting at his desk, twirling his side curls with one hand and thumbing his nose at the black-coated teacher's back with the other. The audience laughed and clapped in appreciative recognition.

I felt good. I could tell that my timing was exactly right by the laughter I got whenever the little Chassid tricked his teacher, or quickly outsmarted him. Grisha never had to prompt me. I even surprised him by putting in a few extra bits of business that he hadn't written into the script. He showed he liked my ad-libbing by quick little nods of his head to me, while he manipulated the teacher on stage in response to the new material. The audience laughed and booed and clapped and stamped their feet, and I was carried away by the excitement of being part of it all.

I was so carried away that at the end of the show, after the audience had cheered and clapped and called us back for a dozen curtain calls, I jumped the little Chassid onto his teacher's back, quite taking poor Grisha by surprise. But he recovered and gamely trotted the teacher off stage. The little Chassid rode astride the teacher like a cowboy in a rodeo show, doffing his wide-brimmed black hat graciously to the audience.

Mira had stood to one side of the puppet theatre during the show, playing the accordian for all the songs and dances and whenever the script called for some musical punctuation. Now, she came backstage her face flushed with pleasure.

"Douzhynka," she said, holding her arms out to me. We hugged each other happily, and then I hugged Grisha and Grisha hugged Mira, and when we were all finished hugging, we started on a second round.

"The little one is very good," said Grisha, patting my head fondly. "You have much talent, very much. Together we make very good show."

"Horoshow," said Mira nodding her head affectionately, and kissing me first on one cheek and then the other.

Under the watchful eyes of the custodian, the audience was leaving, everyone putting something into the copper kettle on the way out. Even the littlest child got something from his parent's purse to put into the pot. Grisha's friends Miron and Verutchka came backstage to congratulate us, and reported that the pot was full to overflowing.

When everybody had finally left, the custodian turned the kettle upside down on the table and divided the money into piles. Paper money in one pile, pounds in another, then half pounds, and finally all the agorot. When we counted the money, we had four hundred and fifty pounds.

"Not bad for one evening," said the custodian, pocketing his share.

Grisha excitedly invited Miron and Verutchka to come out and celebrate the evening with us at a café. We packed the puppets into their plastic shopping bag, and decided to go to the Café Atara, which has the best ice-cream sundaes in all of Jerusalem.

16

We left the little puppet the-atre with the custodian at his suggestion. He was already making plans for another show.

"Don't worry, don't worry, you can leave it here with me—then you won't have to go to the trouble of bringing it back the next time." He was carefully depositing coins into a fat leather purse. Then he looked up at me and smiled. "Oh I like this little Chassida," he said. "She is very good for business," and he patted the pocket of his trousers which now bulged with his share of the evening's take.

Grisha conferred with Mira, and then he turned to me.

"Would you like to repeat the performance in two weeks?" he asked. "In the meantime we could start work on a new show." I nodded happily. The sooner I could get together enough money for fare back home, the better, and it looked as though I was really going to do it! The custodian locked Mira's accordian and the puppets in a closet to be picked up the next day. Then we were ready to leave.

The three of us were elated by our success. We walked down Ben Yehuda to Café Atara arm in arm, Mira humming contentedly, Verutchka and Miron a few paces behind us. It was cool and pleasant out, late enough for the chach-chachim and their girl friends to have left the area. I felt so absolutely lovely that even shabby Ben Yehuda Street looked beautiful to me.

Café Atara was crowded with Saturday-night people. As we waited for a table, a woman turned and stared at me in a puzzled way. I recognized Mom's friend Mitzie, and averted my face, but not quickly enough.

"Josie," she called, "where's your mother? Are you here alone?"

"No," I answered, "I'm here with friends. Mom's in Tel Aviv, but she knows I'm here," I lied.

Oh God! Would she be angry if she knew I was in Café Atara at eleven o'clock at night! And she would just about blow her top if she knew about the money we had collected at the puppet show—or even had an inkling of what I intended to use it for! I nodded and smiled at Mitzie, even though my back was suddenly drenched with sweat, and the whole place and the people in it seemed all at once terribly unattractive.

A group of loud-mouthed American tourists distracted Mitzie just as the waitress found us a table in the back room. I sort of slouched down in my chair and looked around apprehensively to see if anyone else might recognize me. Automatically I started whispering, "Jesus loves me. . . ."

I've gotten into this nervous habit in Mrs. Farrell's class of repeating the hymn over and over under my breath. It all started during those rapid-fire oral examinations she loves to give where she suddenly fixes some poor idiot with a gimlet eye, and says, "Compare the themes of brotherhood in *The Hobbit, The Epic of Gilgamesh,* and *The Iliad.*" I sit there clammily waiting for her to pounce on me with some equally delightful brain scrambler, and I whisper over and over,

> Jesus loves me! this I know,
> For the Bible tells me so;
> Little ones to Him belong,
> They are weak, but He is strong.
> Yes, Jesus loves me,
> Yes, Jesus loves me,
> Yes, Jesus loves me,
> The Bible tells me so.

If I can go through the chorus three times without being called on, I figure I'm safe. Somehow, it's always worked out that way. And it's really a lot better than what I used to do when I nervously expected to be called on, which was to sit there and pluck out my eyebrows. Mom practically had a fit when she noticed that my eyebrows were almost gone. "For God's sake, what are you doing to yourself," she yelled. "Without eyebrows your face looks like a hard-boiled egg!" I guess it did.

Anyway, I was sitting there hunched over with my lips moving, when I caught Miron staring at me. I stopped, and pretended to get terribly interested in the menu. When the waitress came, I ordered a strawberry ice-cream sundae, but somehow, when it arrived, it wasn't really what I wanted.

"I know what you were saying to yourself," said Miron teasingly. "You were planning how much ice cream to buy with your share of the money."

"No I wasn't," I said, not even bothering to be annoyed. It is just so tiresome to always have people treat you like a baby.

"Well, what are you planning to do with your share?"

"Buy a ticket to New York," I said, a spoonful of ice cream halfway to my mouth. I had been going to say, "One for Mira too," but caught myself in time.

Miron opened his eyes wide. "You want to leave?" he asked. "You don't like it here?"

"It's not that I don't like it here," I began. Then I stopped. How could I possibly explain to him. Miron was not like most of the Russian immigrants. Mom had gotten involved with a group of Russians, mostly artists and musicians, when we first came to Israel. I had heard her complaining to Boris about their lack of idealism.

"They come here expecting to be given all sorts of things that they never would have had in a lifetime in Russia. Cars, refrigerators, washing machines, televisions. Everything handed to them by the Israeli government. They even complain about the size of the bedrooms in the apartments they are given, when you know that back in Russia the whole family lived, ate, and slept together in one tiny room!"

"Give them a chance," Boris answered. "It's all new to them. They're like children with toys."

"Don't you believe it! These are no children. They are extremely cynical people. And they can't wait to leave. They just use Israel as a stepping-stone to get out of Russia."

But I knew Miron wasn't like that. He left a very good job in Moscow to become a low-grade laboratory assistant at Hadassah. Because he is single, the government would not give him an apartment, and he will have to stay in that tiny squalid room at Moadon Rasco indefinitely. But he still loves being here. He is hoping that his mother, whom he adores, will be able to get a visa and join him soon.

Suddenly, I felt like a spoiled brat. I wanted to tell him that what I missed wasn't the big house in America, or the swimming pool, or any of the rest of the material things. I just missed being where I had a sense of belonging, being where I wanted to be. I wanted to tell him what it felt like being dragged around like so much excess baggage. That all my mother's talk of this being such a great experience for me didn't help. That I didn't fit in any place, couldn't get comfortable, except with Mira.

I looked across at Mira. She and Grisha had ordered waffles, he with fruit topping, she with syrup, and they were trading off bites.

"Mira doesn't like it here either," I said to Miron. She

didn't. I had seen her get all teary-eyed whenever she thought of Moscow in the snow. "I know Mira isn't happy here," I repeated. "She misses Moscow terribly."

Miron looked over at Mira, and smiled and shrugged his shoulders. "Do you think so?" he asked. She had just given Grisha a spoonful of waffle dripping with syrup, and he was offering her a spoonful of his fruit topping in return. "Maybe she doesn't miss Moscow so much anymore," said Miron. "She looks happy now that she and Grisha have found each other."

I felt my stomach get all tight. "Here, try this, Mira," I said loudly. I shoved a spoonful of strawberry ice cream at her, practically forcing Grisha's fruit topping away. She looked at me, surprised, but accepted my offering.

"It's very good, Douzhynka," she said. "Tov meod," and turned back to Grisha.

I pushed back my chair. "I want to go home, Mira. Home." I wanted to get her away quickly, to try to tell her how happy we were going to be together in America.

"Rega," she said patting my head soothingly. "Rega achad." She could see I was upset.

Everything suddenly seemed impossible to me. My stomach hurt in earnest now, and I thought I was going to throw up. Verutchka was looking at me. "Don't you feel well?" she asked. "Is something wrong?"

"I just want to go home," I answered, not daring to lift my eyes to hers, because the tears might come flooding out.

Miron looked at his watch. "It is time we left," he said to Verutchka. "We will miss the last bus to Moadon

Rasco." The waitress came and gave us the check. We all got up to leave.

"Are you coming with us?" Verutchka asked Grisha as we walked out into the now chilly air.

"No," said Grisha. "I will take the ladies home first."

"You'll miss the last bus to your place," I said to him. "Mira and I can get home alone. We've done it before."

"But not at such a late hour," said Grisha. "It is not right to send two such lovely and talented ladies off by themselves. I will take a taxi home. After all, I can afford it. Tonight's performance has made me a rich man." He took a handful of five-pound notes out of his pocket, and flourished them jokingly.

We caught the bus on King George across from Fink's restaurant. It was the last bus of the evening, and very crowded. I was separated from Mira and Grisha by a very fat lady with a hairy wart on her chin, and I stared at it miserably all the way home.

The walk from the bus stop past the convent wall was silent. When we got to my door, Mira kissed me good night on the cheek. But I turned my face as Grisha leaned toward me, and his kiss landed on my hair.

᪥

17

᪥

The apartment had a stale, closed-in smell when I opened the door. I adjusted the trissim to let the cool night air in, and went out on the balcony before getting into my nightgown. But although I saw all of Mira's lights go out, I didn't see Grisha leave. He must have gone over to Derek Hebron as soon as he'd taken Mira to her door, and caught a cruising taxi. I sat out on the balcony for quite a while looking at the pale moonlit landscape. The odor of jasmine wafted up on the night air, and all of Jerusalem lay sleeping, bleached bone white by the moon.

Finally, I went in, put on my nightgown, and got into bed. But I couldn't fall asleep. From the encampment on the hills overlooking the wadi where the Arab shepherds had tethered their flocks, came the thin clear sound of goats' bells. I lay there listening to them, wondering when

Mom would come home, wondering what Mitzie would tell her, wondering what she would say when she found out I was in town so late.

I began to go over and over the problem of getting Mira to America. The problem of explaining things to her. Things like selling her belongings, like saving the money from the puppet shows for plane fare, like leaving Israel. I kept making up scenes in a play where there were just two characters, Mira and me. But in each of the scenes, after I had gone through the whole business of telling Mira everything, I could see that she really hadn't understood, and I would start again.

I was exhausting myself, but I couldn't stop, couldn't fall asleep. It was as though I had triggered something in my head that I had no control over. Finally, I turned on the bedside light, and picked up a book. That was a mistake, because the book just happened to be *Farmer Boy*, and I just happened to open it to one of those mouthwatering descriptions of the food Almanzo is so fond of. All the *Little House* books make me hungry when I read them, but *Farmer Boy* makes me so hungry that I start salivating. There I was, at three o'clock in the morning, reading how Almanzo "ate the sweet, mellow baked beans. He ate the bit of salt pork that melted like cream in his mouth. He ate mealy boiled potatoes, with brown ham-gravy."

There was nothing much in the refrigerator to snack on. Just a couple of tired-looking sardines in congealed oil, sitting in the little can they'd come in. An overripe avocado, its skin all blackened. Some butter, half out of its wrapper. A few hard old braided rolls. A half-full plastic bag of milk. In the cupboard, I found some packages of Telma: tomato with rice, and mushoom barley.

I fixed myself a cup of tomato-rice soup, then mashed the sardines and avocado with a little onion and lemon juice and spread the mixture on the braided roll which I had buttered and toasted. Not bad, really. I sat at the kitchen table and read about Almanzo demolishing plum preserves and spiced watermelon-rind pickles and large pieces of pumpkin pie, while I demolished my own little feast. Then, feeling quite full, I went back to bed and tried to stay awake till Mom came home. But I fell asleep so soundly that I didn't even hear her come in.

I woke up to the sound of the muezzin calling the faithful to early-morning prayers. It was still dark out, and the air coming in through the half-opened trissim had a hint of dew in it. The shepherds on the hill were playing some flutey instruments and beating on drums. The same kind, I thought, I had used in our parade; made of red clay, shaped like a vase with a long narrow throat that flares out to a goatskin head. I had never heard the lilting sound of the flutes and the wailing of the muezzin together before. It couldn't be Ramadan, I thought sleepily, and started to drift off again.

Suddenly I was fully awake. With all the other sounds in the air, I don't know what made me aware of a faint kind of scrabbling on the marble floor that made my flesh creep. The pale pre-dawn light coming in through the half-open trissim was just enough to allow me, as I lifted my head cautiously, to make out the horrid shape of a scorpion on the floor quite close to my bed.

"M–O–M," I yelled.

There was no answer.

"M–O–O–M!" I wailed, competing with the muezzin. She still didn't hear me.

The only thing to do was to get out at the bottom of the bed, as far away as possible from that evil-looking thing which moved in such a loathsome crawly way, and make a run for Mom's room. I inched my way down to the far end of the bed, keeping my eyes glued to the floor. About halfway there, my hand touched something furry, and I recoiled and let out a piercing shriek. I turned to see Teddy, his beady glass eyes gleaming in the faint light. I grabbed him, swung my legs over the edge of the bed, and ran.

There is something about the way a scorpion scutters along that makes you want to keep yourself up off the floor as high as you can. I ran, lifting my feet with each step as though I were on hot coals. I sprinted down the hall and burst into Mom's room at the far end. It was empty, the bed still made. She had never come home.

Now I was really petrified. If only I could get to Mira! I crouched in the middle of Mom's bed hugging Teddy, my feet tucked under me, half expecting the scorpion to come after me. I longed for Mira's kitchen, for Mira getting me a cup of tea, for just Mira.

After a while, I started to think of ways of getting out of the apartment. The front door was out of the question, I had to go down the length of the dim hallway past my bedroom where the scorpion was to get to it. But I could get out on the balcony and as soon as it got light, yell across to Mira. The sun was beginning to come up, and there was just enough light filtering through the trissim to give me courage.

Clutching Teddy, I ran out of Mom's room and across the living room, pulled the trissim up, and whipped out onto the balcony. Then I quickly dropped the trissim. Now there was a barrier between me and the scorpion and I felt relatively safe. All I had to do was sit on the balcony and wait till the sun was all the way up. I huddled in a rattan chair, chilly and yawning in the early-morning damp.

The garbage collectors came and went, the trucks grinding and clashing their teeth, the men clanking the empty cans back down on the sidewalk. A few skinny Jerusalem cats appeared from nowhere, and sniffed at the garbage cans. Some Arab construction workers carrying woven plastic shopping bags, their heads wrapped in kaffiyehs, passed on their way to the site of the new apartment building down the street. A flock of goats straggled up over the hill near the convent wall, their bells tinkling merrily, followed by a young Arab goatherd. An old Arab walked his faggot-laden donkey down Derek Hebron toward the Old City, twitching him occasionally with a pointed stick, the donkey braying loudly in protest. The convent bells requested the nuns to cease whatever they were doing, and start doing something else. The bright sun was up in a sapphire blue sky, and all of Jerusalem was awake.

Abu Rauchi came out of the doorway of Mira's still-unfinished apartment house, looking dapper and as though he had not spent the night in a bomb shelter.

"Keef haleck," he salaamed gravely to me, as I got ready to somehow tell him to call Mira. Before I could think of the right motions to make, he turned and salaamed again to a familiar figure that had appeared in the doorway behind him.

"Keef haleck," he said, and Grisha, smiling and nodding in return, said "Boker tov!" "Good morning!" and strode off briskly, to catch the bus home.

❧§❧

18

❧§❧

$\mathcal{M}$om came home at about seven o'clock that Sunday morning. As she got out of the taxi, a couple of civilian guards just going off duty, their Uzis slung over their shoulders, walked by.

"Shalom, Geverit."

"Shalom," she answered. She paid the taxi driver, and started along the path to our apartment house.

"Shalom, Geveriti." They smiled up at me.

Her eyes followed theirs, and she saw me huddled in the corner of the balcony above her.

"What are you doing awake so early?" she asked, looking up at me with a kind of false brightness. "Today is Yom Rishon, remember? You don't have to go to school." Her mascara was a little smudged, and her makeup looked harsh in the morning sunlight.

"I've been waiting up for you," I answered. "I woke

up in the middle of the night, and there was a scorpion in the room, and I was all alone. You said you'd be home last night."

"I know, Jo-Jo baby. But I couldn't make it back from Tel Aviv until so late, it didn't seem worth it. Especially since I knew you weren't going to school this morning. I thought you'd still be asleep."

She went in the front door of the apartment house, and I could hear her walking up the marble steps to our door. Then I heard the sound of her key in the lock, and her footsteps as she came in. I didn't budge, just sat in the rattan chair on the balcony. Let her come to me.

"Good morning, Jo-Jo baby." She leaned over and kissed me. The sudden smell of nectarines and raspberries brought back fleetingly times when I was little and everything was different.

"Come," she said. "Show me where the scorpion is and I'll get rid of it. Then we'll have breakfast and get some sleep. I guess we both need it."

Tears of resentment welled up in my eyes. "Why wasn't it worth it—getting back from Tel Aviv? I hate to wake up all alone. It feels horrible."

"I know, Josie. I felt rotten about it all the way home. I promise I won't stay out all night again. Really. I promise."

"It was awful, just awful. I woke up and there was this horrible noise, and I looked down and there was this THING. And when I ran to get you, you weren't there."

"I'm so sorry, sweetie, truly I am." She knelt down and put her arms around me. "Please try to forgive me. I know it's a lousy feeling to depend on someone and find they're not there when you need them." She hugged me, but I didn't hug her back. After a while, she sighed, and said, "Look, we better do something about the scorpion so we can eat and get some rest. I'm terribly tired and I know you must be too."

"Yes, I'm tired. Tired of waiting for you to come home all the time. Tired of feeling as though you don't care about me."

"Oh Josie, Josie baby. I do feel so bad about this. But you must know that I care about you. Just because I didn't get home last night doesn't mean I don't care. I worried about you, and thought of calling when I realized I wouldn't make it back to Jerusalem. But I thought you'd be asleep, and that a phone call would wake you up and frighten you." She put her face against my hair, and stroked my cheek. "Josie, I do love you very very much." She knelt there, just softly stroking my cheek, and after a while the tight feeling inside me loosened up a little bit.

"Come," she said, "let's go in."

I went into the house with her. She got the rug beater that Aida uses, and walking stealthily, we went down the hallway to my room. I hung back at the doorway. "I'm not going in there," I whispered. We both stood at the door and peered in.

"There he is," Mom said pointing. The scorpion hadn't moved much. It was nestled in the corner of the bed-clothes where I'd thrown them off the bed the night before. Mom walked into the room very calmly, and brought the rug beater down hard on the scorpion, making a beastly scrunching sound.

"It must have been awful being alone in the house with that all night," she said as she wiped up the remains with some paper towels.

"I hated it! I was so scared! I bet when you were my age you never woke up to find yourself all alone with a scorpion!"

"No, I never did," she said.

"And don't tell me it's a great experience, because it isn't! I think it's a stinking experience. I hope I never have to sit out on the balcony all night again with no one but an old teddy bear for comfort, waiting till it's light enough to call Mira."

I stopped. Mira. I had all kinds of confused feelings about Mira. And I didn't want to think about her just then.

"I think it's a horrible experience, and I promise you'll never have to spend the night alone again, sweetie."

She held the paper towel with the squooshed scorpion at arm's length as we walked back to the kitchen. After depositing it in the garbage, she turned to the refrigerator. "Let's see what kind of goodies we can dig up." She wrinkled her nose as she sniffed the milk in the plastic bag. "Why don't you put on your jeans and we'll go down to the makolet the way we used to and get some fresh milk and rolls and stuff."

Mom changed into her jeans too. She must have washed her face because all the makeup was gone, and she looked haggard but somehow younger without it. She put her arm around my shoulders as we went down the stairs. It had been a long time since we walked down the road to the store together, not since Boris's last concert tour. The tightness inside me seemed to dissolve and went away completely.

The makolet man was busy waiting on someone else, but he smiled and greeted Mom like an old friend. "I haven't seen you in a long time," he said. Mom chatted with him while he finished taking care of his other customer, and I went and sat on an old orange crate in the doorway.

I come to the makolet pretty often for milk and rolls and things that Mom has forgotten to get at Supersol. But I guess I never bothered to look around before. Now, I was so tired it seemed as though somebody else were looking out of my eyes.

The makolet sits high on a hill, the same one that the shepherds had pitched their tent on the night before. You walk down a few steps off the road, an ordinary enough Jerusalem road. There, quite suddenly, as you step onto the sandy path to the door, laid out before you, looking as though all time—past, present, and future—is contained in it, is the wadi. The hills cascading down to it are a jumble of clay-colored slabs of rock and boulders. They have been there since always; will be there till always. The tawny wrinkled hills that encircle it, one behind the other, going as far as the eye can see, all the way to the mountains of Moab, change colors with the sun. Birds were flying way down below me as I looked, and I caught my breath.

"It really is something, isn't it?" Mom said gently, putting her arm around me. I was glad that she had not felt the need to say something fancy.

We walked home carrying the heavy plastic shopping bag between us, she holding one handle, me holding the other. I helped spread the Israeli-style breakfast on the table: cheese, yogurt, lachmaniot—crispy Israeli rolls—butter, chopped-up tomatoes and cucumbers, green and black olives, and the fragrant coffee made with cardamom that I had learned to enjoy served with lots of hot milk.

"Tell me what you did yesterday after I left," Mom said to me as we ate.

"Oh, nothing much," I answered not really looking at her. Then I remembered Mitzie. "Well, actually I did go into town."

"Did you walk in?"

"No, I waited till the buses started running."

"You went into town in the evening by yourself?"

"No, actually I went with Mira and Grisha."

There it was. Mira and Grisha. Not quite out in the open for me to look at good and hard, just sticking its head out enough so I would have to think about it.

"It's nice that Grisha comes around so often now that Mira is all alone."

"He has to! We're doing this puppet show and it means lots of rehearsing. And she's not alone, she has me. . . ." My voice trailed off as I realized that I had said more than I meant to.

"Of course she has you, sweetie! Are you doing a puppet show for one of those new-immigrant things they put on? I'd love to come and see it if you are doing a part in it."

I stuffed some olives into my mouth and mumbled something about it not being for a while.

I thought about Grisha coming around often. Well, but he really did have to, because of the puppet show and all.

Mom interrupted my thoughts. "Come Jo-Jo, we won't even bother to wash up now. Let's just put the milk and stuff in the refrigerator, and the dishes in the sink. Then you can get into bed with me the way you used to when you were little."

I helped clear off, and got into my nightgown again. We put the trissim all the way down in Mom's room so that it was dim and quiet, and got into bed. Mom kissed me on the top of the head. "Sleep tight, Josie girl," she whispered.

Just before I dozed off, I turned to her and said, "Mom, do you think it is possible that a lady who is fifty-eight years old or so would still want to make love?"

Mom curled herself around me, and made a noise somewhere between a sigh and a groan.

"Josie," she said sleepily, "why don't we sometime after school tomorrow go over to the library, and you can ask the librarian for a book on geriatrics and sex."

‹§›

19

‹§›

I was late for school the next day. Mom and I had slept through most of Sunday, waking up late in the evening to have some supper, and then going back to sleep again. In the morning when the phone rang, I stumbled out of bed.

"Boker tov. Ha sha'ah reva le sheva." "Good morning. It is quarter to seven," said the wake-up service. I crawled back into bed and fell asleep again.

Mom woke me up about an hour later. "Josie, Josie," she said anxiously shaking my shoulder. "Wake up. I'm afraid we've overslept. You'll be late for school."

I quickly got into my clothes and dashed out the door of our flat, stuffing a buttered roll into my mouth as I ran down the marble steps.

"Josie, here catch this!" Mom was standing above me on the balcony as I ran down the path. She threw down a paper bag with some fruit in it, and I caught it just before it landed on the flagged walk.

When I got to school, everyone was in assembly. I could hear Mrs. Kerujian, the art teacher who plays the piano for assemblies, striking the opening chords for Hymn 606, then the voices singing:

> All things bright and beautiful,
> All creatures great and small,
> All things wise and wonderful,
> The Lord God made them all.
> Each little flower that opens,
> Each little bird that sings—
> He made their glowing colors,
> He made their tiny wings.

I went to the office and got a late-admission slip. Miss Lynton looked down her beaky nose disapprovingly as she wrote it out for me. Then she said, "Josie, is your mother at home today? Mrs. Farrell would like to see her after school."

"What about, Miss Lynton? My Math is improving. Mr. Vandervoss says I'm doing much better now."

"I'm afraid I'm not free to discuss it," said Miss Lynton, handing me the slip of paper.

I went into Mrs. Farrell's room feeling a little sick, and sat down in my seat. I opened my history book and tried to get involved with the Norman Conquest, but the buttered roll in my stomach seemed to be doing push-ups. Everything was very quiet.

After a while the assembly-room doors burst open, and I could hear the hum of voices coming down the hall.

"Hi Josie." Maryanne came in, her face freckled and peeling. "We went to Ashkelon this weekend and my back is all blistered. Did you get to go anywhere?" She breezed past without waiting for an answer.

Stella minced by on bright red platforms.

"Maryanne, wait up for me. I have something to tell you," she called in her sexy voice.

Rosamunda passed on her way to her seat, holding up to her mouth a paper bag with a half-eaten lachmania sticking out of it.

"Oops, sorry!" she said, as a few stray crumbs scattered onto my desk. She picked them up and licked them off her fingertips.

Mathias came in, his first day back in school since his fainting fit. I could feel his presence even before he reached my desk. He didn't say anything, just gave me a long hard sideways look as he passed, but the smug smile on his face as he looked at me made the hackles rise on the back of my neck. Definitely, he was up to something.

Finally, after a long time, Mrs. Farrell came in. She didn't say anything to me when I handed her the late-admission slip, but her thin lips compressed into an even straighter line. She sniffed as though she didn't like what she was smelling, and tucked my pass into her roll book.

"Well class," she said, putting her chalky-dry finger-tips together. "We will begin with a discussion of the Bayeux Tapestry. I would like an exact description of all seventy-two of the scenes depicted on it, starting with the

127

events leading up to the Battle of Hastings. Rajah, would you like to begin, and remember, I want details, please, details."

Immediately, my hand rose to my eyebrows, and I plucked out several hairs before I remembered that *Jesus Loves Me* works better. I could tell it was going to be a bad day.

When the bell rang for recess, Mrs. Farrell said, "Josephina will you come up for a moment. I'd like to talk to you." My legs felt rubbery as I walked to her desk. She never calls me Josephina unless she is really angry, like the time I was in such a hurry to get out of her room that I climbed up on the window ledge and jumped, instead of going out through the door.

"Josephina," she said, "I am asking your mother to come in after school today, and I would like you to be present at that time. Mathias has made some extremely disturbing accusations against you, and I think you have the right to be there when I speak to your mother."

I couldn't believe my ears. "Mrs. Farrell," I began, "I don't know what Mathias said about me but—"

"That will do," she said. "You may go out for recess now."

I went out into the bright sunlight, and sat down on the pile of rocks under the eucalyptus tree. Maryanne and Stella were standing off in a corner talking to Rajah and Carlos. Rosamunda and Catherine were playing Hamesh Avanim. I picked up a small rock from the pile I was sitting on. It seemed odd that it looked no different from a rock I might pick up on our driveway in Connecticut, six thousand miles away.

Suddenly, a shadow fell on the rock in my hand. "I fix you good, yes?" Mathias was standing behind me, and if I didn't know any better, I would really think from the look on his face at that moment that he adored me.

"Leave me alone, Mathias, please," I said, getting up and moving away.

Maryanne called over to me, "Josie, is that pest after you again?"

"I do not pester her," said Mathias. "She provokes me. She makes me ill. I faint through her provoking me."

"What!" yelped Maryanne. "You're bonkers, you are! She was nowhere around when you fainted. Jenine El Gazi was walking right in back of you when you keeled over, and she told me it was all a big fake anyway."

"Fake, fake, what is this fake. I faint because I was made ill by her."

"I bet that's what Mrs. Farrell wants to see my mother about," I said to Maryanne. "She's asked her to come in after school today because of something Mathias said."

"Yess, yess. Mrs. Farrell knows now the truth, as does Mr. Vandervoss. They both know now the truth. But our Lord, He always knows the truth." He moved away, looking like some evil dwarf.

"He reminds me of a dirty joke," said Maryanne looking after him. "But it was such a bad one, I've forgotten it. Look, if you want me to tell your Mum how much he pesters you, I will. I'll even tell Mrs. Farrell that he's the one who is always after you, not the other way around. O.K.?"

"Maryanne," said Stella, "I really don't think you should get yourself involved in this."

"Well, I just don't think it's fair. Someone ought to tell Josie's mother how rotten Mathias is to her."

"Thanks, Maryanne," I said. "But I don't see how you can help unless you see my mother before Mrs. Farrell gets to her."

"Well, why can't I do that? I'll meet her at the gate after school, and tell her how Mathias torments you, and how he's blaming you for his stupid fainting fit when you weren't even there, and how he got Mrs. Farrell and Mr. Vandervoss believing him."

"Oh, Maryanne, I wish you'd stay out of this," said Stella. "Anyhow, you've never met Josie's mother. How will you know who she is?"

"I know what Josie's mother looks like. I saw her when she came to *Joseph's Technicolor Dream Coat*. She has long dark straight hair, way below the shoulders, and she doesn't wear the kind of clothes that other mothers wear. Don't worry, I'll spot her."

I felt a little better as we walked into Math class after recess. But it didn't last long. Mr. Vandervoss was back, the first time he had put in an appearance since escorting Mathias out to Beit Jallah. He started us off with an oral quiz, "To refresh your memory of all the work we have done." He went rapid fire down the rows of desks, calling on people. At any other time, I would have been glad that he skipped right past me. But today I had the distinct impression that he was going out of his way to overlook me.

Lunch was pretty dismal. I sat in a corner eating the fruit out of the paper bag that Mom had thrown down, and wondering what Mathias could possibly have said to Mrs. Farrell to make her believe him.

After lunch, we had English, then Science, then Hebrew. Mrs. Farrell is our main teacher. We have her every day for History and English, and three times a week for Science. Occasionally, she fills in for the Art and Scripture teachers when they are absent. Usually, I sort of like her. Her strict prim old-lady ways give me a kind of nice secure feeling. With Mrs. Farrell you always know what to expect. She has very definite opinions that you can rely on. But today, I couldn't bear to look at her during English and Science. She was prim and prissy and opinionated all right, and totally unfair! The hours dragged by so slowly that I kept thinking the clock on the wall over her desk must have stopped.

Finally it was Hebrew, with Miss Zipporah drilling us in pa-al, nif-al, pi-el, poo-al, hif-el, hoof-al, hit-pa-el.

"I'll go down and meet your mother now," Maryanne said to me as soon as we left Miss Zipporah's room. She squeezed my hand sympathetically. "Don't worry, Josie. I'm sure it will all sort itself out."

I went into Mrs. Farrell's room, feeling a little like a criminal who has already been judged.

Mrs. Farrell was standing behind her desk. She was busily arranging books, putting some into her shopping bag, making neat piles of others. She looked up as I came in.

"Oh, there you are," she said. "Miss Lynton has been

trying to get your mother on the phone all day. But she hasn't been able to reach her." She picked up an envelope from her desk, and handed it to me. "I've written a note asking that she come in tomorrow at noon. Will you please see that she gets it?"

I walked down the graveled path to the gate scuffing my feet in the stones. Why couldn't Mom have been home today? When I'd left this morning, I'd felt so close to her. Well, so much for being there when I needed her. Boris had probably called, and she'd gone off with him.

⛤

20

⛤

$\mathcal{M}$aryanne turned as she heard my approaching footsteps. "Your Mum's very late," she said. "Mrs. Farrell isn't going to like that."

"She's not coming," I answered. "Mrs. Farrell wants her to come tomorrow instead."

"Oh, honestly Josie, don't look so upset. It's really better this way. I'll call you at home tonight and you can put me through to her. I know once I've told your mother what Mathias is like, she'll come in here and give 'em all what for! Don't you see, pet? It will be so much easier than if I tried to tell her about it down here at the gate while old lady Farrell sits up there waiting."

"I suppose you're right," I answered. "But still, I wish she'd been home."

"She's probably home by now," said Maryanne. "I've got to go. I'll call you later."

I hurried to the bus stop. Maryanne was right. Mom probably was home by now. She would have told me this morning if she had intended to be out all day. I waited impatiently in the queue. When the bus finally came, it was terribly crowded. A pregnant woman carrying a cute curly-headed kid tried to get the kid's pram onto the bus. She was offered a seat, and three men jumped off and folded the pram, but still couldn't get it on. Just my luck, when I was anxious to get home as quickly as possible.

All the passengers were craning their necks to watch the action.

"Try it sideways, sideways," directed the man standing next to me.

"It wouldn't help," said a woman behind us. "You don't see? The handle sticks out too far."

"So, no problem, we take the handle off. Bus driver, where's your tool kit? We need a screw driver."

The bus driver had his head out the window directing traffic which was piling up behind us. A schoolboy started acting as a go-between, taking orders and delivering refreshments from the kiosk on the corner, doing a brisk business through the open windows. "Nu, so what flavors does he have? Only orange and grapefruit?"

"Would you be so kind as to pass the change back. Also the empty bottle?"

I shifted around in what space I had, wishing they'd get on with it. The curly-headed kid started to cry. Someone offered him a swig of orange soda, and he spit it out all over his mother.

"Come, I'll hold him for you," said the man sitting

next to her. He had a watch on, and as he reached for the kid I tried to see what time it was. There was a serial number tattooed in blue on the tanned skin above his watch. Auschwitz? Bergen-Belsen? I had been to Yad Va Shem, the memorial to the Jews who died in the holocaust, had seen the photographs, had looked in all the glass cases, knew the names of the concentration camps.

He cradled the kid gently in his arms, and looked up at me. "What's your hurry?" he said mildly, as though he'd read my mind. "There's always plenty of time to help someone, plenty of time."

Meanwhile, the men with the pram had gotten a ladder from a storekeeper and were performing some sort of balancing act; one man on the ladder, two juggling the pram. Someone inside the bus opened the ventilation hatch in the roof.

"Oopla!" The man on the ladder swung the pram up and lowered it through the hatch. The whole bus cheered, and I breathed a sigh of relief as the bus started to roll again. Little curly head was asleep on the lap of the mild-mannered man. One of his tiny fists resting on the bronzed arm obscured the first two numbers of the tattoo.

"You see." The man was smiling up at me. "It did not take so long after all."

For the second time that week I felt like a spoiled brat. I hated him for making me hate myself.

When I got home I found a pile of groceries outside the door of the flat where the delivery boy from Supersol had dumped them. So Mom had been out shopping. She must have expected to get home before the delivery truck did. She wouldn't want the milk and butter to sit on the landing for any length of time.

I opened the front door and carried in the milk. The note on the kitchen table said, "Jo-Jo, will be back shortly. Put the groceries away if they get here before I do." Next to the note was a pile of books. So she'd been to the library too.

The top book on the pile was *More out of Sex After Sixty*, by Drs. Crokett and Kraus. Under that was *The Best Is Yet to Come—Sex After Menopause*, by Effie Blight, and *Prime Time—Sex in the Middle Years*, by Hugh F. Jolly. I opened *Sex After Sixty*. There was a photo in the front of a pretty smug-looking elderly couple, Crokett and Kraus. It would be a long while before anyone put those two into a nursing home. Crokett, the lady, was very chic and hard and skinny, and her teeth were exceptionally long and white. Plastic, probably. I thought of Mira, who is all warm and soft and definitely not chic, and whose two front teeth gleam silver. As soon as I thought of her, I needed to see her.

I put the groceries away quickly, and ran across the street. Abu Rauchi smiled at me and pointed upstairs as though to indicate that Mira was waiting. I ran up the steps two at a time. When I got to Mira's landing, I paused a second to catch my breath.

"Mira," I heard a voice speaking very slowly. "It's wonderful, wunderbar, maksim. Josie will be thrilled." It was Mom's voice, very loud and clear through the door, like she was talking to someone who was deaf and dumb and simpleminded.

I walked in without waiting for Mira to answer my knock. Mom and Mira were sitting at the kitchen table. Mom was holding a cup of tea in one hand. With the other she seemed to be trying to conduct an orchestra, using a cookie for a baton. The large sweeping gestures were supposed to help Mira understand. Mira was following the hand gestures a little like someone watching a Ping-Pong match.

"Mom," I said, "that's unnecessary really. You don't have to shout or use hand signals. How come you're up here, anyway? You never visited Mira before."

"Douzhynka!" Mira turned and greeted me as though she hadn't seen me in weeks. Her warm welcoming smile wasn't a bit plastic, and I snuggled into her outstretched arms. Mom leaned over and kissed me.

"Hi, Jo-Jo. I met Mira while I was out shopping, and she invited me up for a cup of tea. How was school today?"

"Awful," I answered, still snuggled into Mira's arms. "Mrs. Farrell wants to see you tomorrow at noon."

Mom lifted her eyebrows. "Really?" she said. "What's up?"

"That boy. You know. The one who's always pestering me. He told Mrs. Farrell that I did something terrible to him and she believes him."

Mira squeezed me a little. "Do you want tea?" she whispered in Hebrew, and got up to give me a cup.

"I can't understand why she'd believe him without some proof," Mom said.

"Oh, Mom. There you go again. Do you actually think I did really do something to him?"

"Josie, I didn't say that! I'm wondering why a woman in a position of authority, who should weigh everything before coming to a conclusion, would believe this boy without hearing your side."

"I don't know, Mom. I suppose he put on a good enough act to convince her. But Maryanne has promised to stick up for me. She says she's willing to tell Mrs. Farrell that Mathias is the one who does all the plaguing and pestering. She's going to call later and you can talk to her."

Mira came back with my tea, and poured another cup for Mom.

"Mrs. Farrell seemed such a nice lady the night I came to see you in the play," Mom mused. "Isn't her husband stationed here as a UN Observer?"

"Oh Mom, how could that possibly matter. What difference does it make if her husband's a UN Observer or a pinball-machine salesman?"

"No difference," said Mom. "I was just hoping she didn't get her sense of fairness from him."

"Listen Mom," I said suddenly alarmed. "You're not going to say anything funny tomorrow, are you?"

"No, of course not, Josie. I wouldn't dream of it."

"That's good," I said relieved. I reached for a cookie. "Now what were you trying to tell Mira when I came in?"

"Oh, I was just trying to tell her how pleased you'd be to help her give a party."

"A party? What kind of a party?"

"Well, I haven't gotten it straight yet, but I'm getting closer. When I met Mira at Hamashbier she was obviously shopping for a party. She had gotten together a whole bunch of things like those little crepe-paper baskets that you put candy in, and all sorts of other party doodads. I told her your birthday wasn't for several months, but she says it's not for you. So that's what we've been talking about."

Mira, who had been listening intently, now went into the other room and brought back a shopping bag. She spilled some of the contents out onto the table, and sure enough, she definitely had some sort of party in mind. It struck me that I knew what it was all about. It had something to do with the puppet shows of course. She and Grisha had decided to give a proper party, and invite all their Ulpan and Moadon Rasco friends. If she splurged on refreshments the way she had on party decorations, it would take forever to save up enough money for her plane ticket!

"Mira," I started to say, "you and Grisha . . ." Then I realized that Mom was listening and I'd better be careful.

"Ken, ken, yes, yes," Mira said, smiling radiantly and shaking her head in vigorous agreement.

"Oh how nice!" said Mom. "Mira and Grisha, how nice! And she looks so happy too! Mira," Mom spoke very loudly and slowly. "I am very glad. It is good!"

"Is good," repeated Mira, her cheeks glowing. "Horoshow!"

"Mom," I said impatiently, "you really do have a one-track mind. Mira is not that Crokett lady. I mean you can tell just from looking at her."

"What Crokett lady?" Mom asked.

"The one in the book. You know. Crokett and Kraus. *Sex After Sixty.*"

"Josie, I don't understand why you feel you have exclusive rights to Mira. Don't you think it's possible that if you found her sweet and kind and gentle, Grisha might have found her so too?"

All this time, Mira had been straining to follow the conversation. I looked over at her now, wondering how much of it she had understood. She smiled at me gently, looking very wise and kind. Of course Grisha might feel that way about Mira. But that didn't mean that Mira felt that way about him. I got up and started to clear the tea things. "I think we ought to go home now," I said. "Maryanne's supposed to call."

Mom and I washed up while Mira packed the party stuff back into the shopping bag. I would have to sit down very soon and talk to her. Somehow I had to explain to her about saving her money for a plane ticket so we could go to America. As for Grisha, I didn't really see that he fit in at all.

≈§₴≈

21

≈§₴≈

"Will your mother be coming in at noon today?" asked Mrs. Farrell after assembly the next morning. She brushed an imaginary wrinkle out of her skirt, and patted her neatly combed hair.

"Yes, Mrs. Farrell," I said, half hoping that Mom wouldn't show up. Maryanne had called last night. She had told Mom exactly how Mathias acted. How he pestered and bullied and in general made life miserable for me when he had half a chance. Mom was really furious by the end of the conversation.

"I don't understand how Mrs. Farrell could have ignored all this," she said. "And I wish you had told me what was going on before it reached this point."

"Oh sure, Mom. The one time I did tell you anything about what was going on, you pulled this business of how Mathias couldn't be acting like that because he is German, and Germans didn't ever do creepy things anymore. I mean when I tried to tell you that it is just coincidence that he is German, that mostly he is just a rotten perverted idiot, you wouldn't really listen."

"I don't think we need go into why I didn't believe this boy was carrying on in such a wretched way. The point is, I wasn't there to see it happen, but Mrs. Farrell was."

"Mom, Mathias doesn't ever do anything in front of Mrs. Farrell. He may be a creep, but he's not stupid. He's never once done anything when any of the teachers could see him. That's how he gets me into trouble. They hear me yelling the way I did when he hit me with a steel ruler, and they get angry at me."

"Well," said Mom, "I certainly intend to find out why Mrs. Farrell didn't know what was really going on. She should have made it her business to get to the bottom of it with scrupulous fairness. And her husband was sent here as a member of a commission of objective observers, God help us!"

"Now Mom, you promised you wouldn't say anything funny! Please, you're just going to make it worse for me." I hoped to God she wasn't going to harp on Mrs. Farrell's husband and the UN and say something really embarrassing.

I don't know how I managed to sit through History. By the time recess came around I was a nervous wreck. I had said Jesus Loves Me so many times my brain felt numb, and I had pulled out half my eyebrows besides. Even Maryanne noticed it.

"Gawd, Josie," she said when we were out in the bright light of the play area. "What have you done to yourself? You look kind of all pink and bald around the eyes."

"Oh Maryanne, I just know my mother is going to say something really weird to Mrs. Farrell."

"Don't be silly, Josie. What could she possibly say? Look, she doesn't think you're the one to blame after all that long conversation I had with her yesterday. And anyway, I'm going to be there when you go in to see Mrs. Farrell. Sort of like a witness for the defense. As soon as the bell rings for lunch, we'll go down and meet your mother at the gate."

I sat under the eucalyptus tree watching the kids play in the bright sunlight; wishing that recess were over, wishing that Math were over, that lunch had come and gone.

Mom showed up promptly at noon. She was wearing a long skirt with a beautiful paisley pattern in mulberry and lavender on a cream background, and a little pale blue cotton top. No bra, of course. Her long black hair hung down very straight as though she'd just washed it. Actually, she looked very nice, but not like any of the other mothers I'd seen at school. Rosamunda's mother looks like a double-chinned dumpling. She wears good sensible clothes that are bought for their lasting qualities rather than style. Her fat little legs end in plain tied shoes that toe in. Maryanne's mother looks an older edition of Maryanne; very pert and jolly, her hair arranged neatly, not fly-about, decent-length skirts, stockings no matter how hot the weather, a standard British mum. Rajah's mother, except for her distinctly Arab face, looks like a suburban mother off for lunch and the weekly bridge game with the girls. And here was Mom, looking, I suddenly realized, like Nefertiti dressed in boutique clothes.

Maryanne seemed to be trying to make a good impression on her, making small talk in a grown-up and boring way. "Terribly hot, isn't it?" she said brightly, opening the car door for Mom.

"Thank you, Maryanne, yes it is," said Mom. Years of studying ballet and modern dance hadn't hurt her figure any. I found myself looking at her through Maryanne's eyes. Not bad, I decided. In fact pretty neat. Then I thought of Mrs. Farrell, and wished she'd at least worn a bra today.

We walked up the graveled path to the school. Mrs. Farrell was waiting in her room very primly, both feet flat on the floor, her fingertips pressed together on the desk before her. A look of disapproval passed over her face when we came in.

"Maryanne," she snapped, "would you please leave."

"She's only here to tell you what she has seen Mathias do to Josie in your classroom without any provocation, and with no interference from you," was Mom's quick comeback.

"I refuse to discuss what goes on in my classroom in the presence of a pupil who is not involved," said Mrs. Farrell, her lips getting thinner and thinner with each word. "Maryanne, you may go now."

Maryanne, looking scared and relieved, left the room.

"Now, Mrs. Hayden," said Mrs. Farrell, "I have asked you to come in because Mathias has been repeatedly annoyed and teased by Josie. On several occasions both Mr. Vandervoss and I have had to reprimand Josie for her actions. But I'm afraid that last week she went a bit too far. She so provoked Mathias that he fainted, and had to be taken home by Mr. Vandervoss."

Mom had gotten pale as Mrs. Farrell spoke, and her eyebrows, which are quite dark against her skin, had lifted higher and higher, until I thought they would disappear under her hair.

"Mrs. Farrell," she said in a carefully controlled voice, "I cannot understand how it is possible for you to have had to reprimand Josie when she has all along been the victim of Mathias's brutal behavior. Josie has been coming home from school for weeks now, with stories of how this boy torments and persecutes her. And yet, not only have you preferred to overlook it, but you are now turning the whole thing around to make Josie appear the aggressor."

"Well, Mrs. Hayden," said Mrs. Farrell; she pressed her fingertips down on the desk so hard that the nails turned white. "I fail to understand why, if you knew Josie was being persecuted, you waited until this moment to tell me. Surely, if as you say, this has been going on for weeks, you would have been in here by now to make some protest. I must say Mrs. Hayden, I find this very hard to believe."

"And I find it very difficult to believe that you could

not or would not see what was going on right under your nose!"

"I did observe what was going on, as you say, 'under my nose.'" She lifted her fingertips. I was surprised to see ten moist spots on the desk where they'd been. Somehow, I thought they would have left dusty chalk marks. "As you know," Mrs. Farrell was saying, "Mathias did faint. And he has said that Josie teased and provoked him to a point that was unendurable."

"I heard all about it. Josie was nowhere present when he fainted. She was getting extra help with her Math from Mr. Vandervoss, and was in his room when it happened. Furthermore, I understand that you were not in the hallway at that time either, but came a few minutes later after one of the students ran to you for help. How can you then believe Mathias when he says Josie made him faint? Surely it is most unfair just to take Mathias's word for it?"

"Mrs. Hayden, I have heard Josie yell and scream and carry on over and over again in my classroom, with Mathias always as the target. I have had to ask her to stop on several occasions when things have gotten out of hand. I can very well believe that she provoked him to a point where he fainted, especially since he is not at all well."

"Mrs. Farrell, it seems to me that Josie has been terrorized by Mathias. That the yelling and screaming have been a direct response to his brutality. That because she committed the indelicacy of showing pain, of letting you know that she was being victimized, you not only turn your head the other way preferring not to see, but call her the terrorist, adding insult to injury! It almost has an all-too-familiar political ring to it!"

Mrs. Farrell was shaking with rage. I don't remember ever seeing her look like that. Even when Carlos and Simeon and Rajah stood up in class on a dare and sang:

We don't care if it rains or freezes
We are safe in the arms of Jesus
And if the world should turn to glass
We'll watch Baby Jesus slide on His ass!

she didn't look quite so angry.

She opened her mouth, then closed it tight again, and slowly surveyed my mother from head to foot. I could feel her taking in the long skirt, the tank top, the bralessness, the straight hair worn much too long for a proper mother. Nothing she saw made her feel any better.

She turned to me. "Josie, you may leave the room now," she said biting off each word. "Your mother and I will continue this discussion without benefit of your presence."

I started to walk out of the room. As I reached the door, I heard Mrs. Farrell say, "Mrs. Hayden, you are eccentric!" That was all I heard. I closed the door carefully behind me, and leaned up against the wall. There was no one in sight. Everyone was still down in the lunchroom most likely. Oh God, how was I ever going to sit through English? Through Science? Through Scripture? Why couldn't she have worn a bra today?

After a while, I went outside and down to the gate and

got in the car. There was no way I was going to stay in school for the rest of the afternoon. I sat on the blazing hot plastic seat wishing I could melt into it, looking at the patterns of sunlight and shadow on the graveled paths. Rippling from dark to light on the grass, bright on the flowers, dark under trees and benches.

Presently, there emerged through the dappled light the figure of my mother. She was walking jauntily, even airily, her bosom bobbing just the least little bit. "When I'm grown up," the thought came out of nowhere, drifting into my head, "maybe I'll walk like that."

"Josie," she said, "I went to the lunchroom to look for you. I'm glad you thought to come down to the car. I've told Mrs. Farrell that you won't be back in school for the rest of the day. We'll go have some lunch now. How about Ta'amon?"

She slid into the front seat without waiting for an answer. We drove to Ta'amon not saying anything much. We parked in the municipal parking lot across the street, and waited patiently for the old Yemenite to give us our ticket and collect the thirty agorot. Then we walked up the stairs into the restaurant. The place has the best humus in town—garlicky, with a few whole chick-peas in the swirl of olive oil on top—so it is always crowded. We found two seats at a table filled with students. The waiter removed the clutter of dirty dishes before us, mopped the table ineffectually with a rag, and slapped down some silverware.

He was about to hustle away, when Mom stopped him. "Soup and humus for two," she said quickly. Then she turned to me. She had a funny quizzical look on her face.

"Josie," she said, "Mrs. Farrell and I never did come to an agreement about this whole miserable business. Although I think that she is much more willing to concede that Mathias might, just possibly might, be the aggressor. But something she said makes no sense at all. Aside from the fact that she made it very clear that I was not a very good mother because you frequently come to school looking what she calls 'tatty,' she thinks that I am utterly delinquent in my duties because I allow you to beg in the streets! I cannot for the life of me understand what would make Mathias swear to something as nutty as the fact that he saw you acting as the main attraction for some organized group of beggars on the Jaffa Road!"

22

"I still don't understand it," Mom was saying. "Do you mean that you were doing the puppet show to raise money? Don't I give you a big enough allowance?" We had finished eating lunch and had driven over to the Jaffa Gate, the entrance to the Old City closest to the butcher shop where Mom gets her meat. She pulled the car up near the gate, facing the high stone wall that surrounds the Old City. The wall was pale gold in the afternoon sunlight, its crenellations biting into the blue of the sky.

Mrs. Farrell had taken our class for a walk on the ramparts once. She'd explained that the Turks built the wall around the Old City with crenellations so that soldiers could hide behind the places that stick up like teeth and be protected, while they shot at the enemy below from the spaces between. I sat there looking at the pale gold against the bright blue.

"You give me enough of an allowance for most things," I answered. "But I really want to save up a whole pile of money. Much more than I can from my allowance."

"What for?" Mom asked, putting the car in reverse and lining it up with the car next to ours.

"Oh, I just want to," I said vaguely.

Immediately we parked, a small Arab boy, about seven or eight years old, ran over with a rag in his hand and started polishing our side-view mirror.

"Lah, lah," said Mom, using the one Arabic word she can say.

He would have given her an argument, but another car pulled up and he hotfooted over to it, hoping for a cash customer. Mom took her straw shopping basket out of the trunk, and we walked to the gate, skirting a stream of water that trickled in the gutter from a cistern.

Some Arab ladies in long black embroidered dresses walked by, baskets of vegetables on their heads. A few old Arabs in rusty black robes, bare brown-skinned feet in down-at-the-heel oxfords, squatted near the gate, sunning themselves. We passed the usual lineup of beggars and international frowsy-headed kids, and followed the cobbled street through the arched gate into the plaza.

The plaza is always filled with parked taxis, police jeeps, and delivery vans. Branching off to the right is the road that leads to the Wailing Wall. Mom and I go there sometimes on Friday nights to watch the Chassidim dance, their arms linked, black frock coats flying, side curls under the broad-brimmed fur hats jiggling, very much like my little puppet.

Straight ahead and down a few steps is the narrow cobbled street with overhead arches that leads to Mom's butcher. Here and there the street is completely roofed over, and the sun filters down dimly through occasional holes. The street is lined with shops selling tourist junk: camel saddles, rugs, glass beads, sheepskin coats, baskets, hand-blown vases, embroidered shirts. The merchandise overflows the shops and is displayed hanging up or piled in the street, leaving a narrower corridor for the crowds to mill in, and accumulating yet another layer of the gray white dust of East Jerusalem. As soon as I walk down that street my nose starts itching from all the fibers and dust and the smell of herbs and spices, and the pissy smell of the public latrines.

"Josie, I really want to understand what is going on in your mind," Mom said. "What do you want all this money for?"

"Allo, allo, allo," warned an Arab, pushing his heavily laden donkey before him through the crowds on the steps. Mom and I were briefly separated by donkey and master, followed by a small boy balancing a large tray of freshly baked bread sprinkled with sesame seeds on his head. When I rejoined her, she was examining an embroidered blouse hung out in front of a shop.

"Welcome, welcome, you are most welcome," we were greeted by Yusaf Barakoush, the owner of a shop where Mom likes to stop and haggle. "Welcome, you are welcome." He bowed very low, and we followed his courtly gesture into the dim interior. "May I offer you coffee, Geverit?" Yusaf is absolutely villainous looking, but he is terribly polite, and Mom always thinks she has gotten a bargain after she has haggled interminably with him over the price of a blouse.

He clapped his hands, and his son Anwar came out from behind a curtain at the back of the shop. Yusaf said something to him in Arabic, and Anwar, after grinning at me, disappeared behind the curtain again. He reappeared minutes later dangling a brass tray suspended by a thin rod from a ring hooked over his forefinger. On the tray were three tiny cups of café Turkit, honey sweet, made with cardamom, and very thick if you try to drink it before it settles. Mom sat on a big hassock Yusaf pushed over for her, and sipped coffee. Anwar was showing me blouses, pulling them out from stacks that were piled ceiling high.

"You like this, you like this," he kept saying. "Why you nervous, why you nervous." I wasn't nervous, except from his bothering me. I wished he would leave me alone, disappear behind the curtain again. But his eyes kept dropping insistently to my shirt where my bosom would be if I had one, as though my face were down there and he was looking for a response from that direction. He got me so confused that when I coughed, I put up my hand and covered my chest instead of my mouth.

Mom and Yusaf were discussing the problems of raising children. Yusaf has a son studying medicine at the University of Chicago. All the Arab merchants in Jerusalem have sons studying to be doctors in the American Midwest. Yemen-on-the-Mississippi. I suddenly had a picture of Anwar floating on a raft with Jim. Anwar Finn.

"It costs much money, very much money," Yusaf was saying. "But we give all for our children. Is that not so, Madame?"

Mom's eyes flicked over to me. "Yes," she said getting up. "Thank you very much for the coffee, Yusaf. We will do business next time I come. Today I must hurry."

"As you wish, Madame, as you wish. You will be most welcome." He bowed us out, not before Anwar, however, had slid his hand caressingly down my departing rear end. I tripped out the door, looking daggers over my shoulder at him, and he grinned at me, the merest tip of his tongue showing pinkly suggestive in the corner of his mouth.

"Josie," Mom said to me, "I want to know about this money thing. All of it. You're not just saving to stuff it under your mattress. There must be something you're saving *for*."

"Why do you always go in there," I said. "That Anwar is disgusting."

"Josie, you're not answering my question. What do you want all that money for?"

"I want to go home," I said.

"We'll go home as soon as I've gone to the butcher."

"No. I mean really home," I said.

"Josie, we've been through this before."

"Well, you want to know what I'm saving money for."

Mom stopped walking and looked at me. "What are you saving for?" she asked.

"I just told you. I want to go home."

She started walking again. "Now let me see if I understand you. You are saving money," she said, "to go home."

We came to the butcher shop. The butcher raises his own pigs. "You are saving money to go home," Mom repeated. There were a few pigs hung from hooks behind the counter. Their fur was a matted dirty gray. I always think of pigs as being fat and pink, but these pigs were skinny and gray. "You mean you are saving money to buy a ticket?" Mom asked.

"Yes," I said miserably, staring at a skinny dead gray pig.

"What are you thinking of doing when you get there?" asked Mom.

"What would you like today, Madame?" asked the butcher.

"How are the steaks?"

"Very good, Madame, the best."

"I was going to live in our house."

"In our house? Yes, I'll have several of those, about three centimeters thick, please. Like about so." She demonstrated with her thumb and forefinger. "How in our house? All by yourself?"

"No," I whispered, transferring my gaze from the pig to some choice entrails displayed on a white marble slab. This is the cleanest butcher shop in the Old City, in all of Jerusalem, according to some people. There were only two flies buzzing around the entrails. The butcher was showing Mom the steaks, fanned out on brown waxed paper.

"Some sausage, Madame? Very good, very fresh."

"Yes, about two hundred grams please. Who did you think you were going to live with?"

I scuffed my foot on the marble floor, and looked through the glass front of the counter into the eye of a lamb. Its severed head was sitting along with those of two other lambs on a spotlessly white shiny tray. This really is a very clean butcher shop.

"With Mira," I answered, unfocusing my eye from the lamb's.

"With Mira. Yes, I'll have one hundred grams of the bacon and two hundred of the ham, please." She turned to me. "With Mira—in the manner to which she would like to become accustomed, no doubt."

"Mom, Mira's not like that. She doesn't even know. I haven't told her."

"You mean Mira is not dying to get to America like all the other Russians? How about Grisha, was he in on this?"

"I never was going to ask Grisha to come with us."

Mom lifted her eyebrows and stared at me. "Whatever made you think that she would be willing to go without Grisha? What made you think that Mira would consent to any of this, or that she would be able to get a visa if she did? And what in God's name did you expect to live on once you got there? Manna from heaven? Josie, you are the most outrageous mixture of grown-up-before-your-time knowledge, and complete childishness I've ever seen!"

"Will there be anything else today, Madame?"

"Yes. No. That is, I'd like to order a large turkey. I'll pick it up on Friday. You are open on Friday? Oh yes,

I forgot. You're not Moslem. You'll have to excuse me. I'm a bit confused."

"Certainly, Madame, certainly. We are Christians, Madame." The butcher was handing her neat brown waxed-paper parcels, tied up with string, that she arranged in her basket. "How big a turkey would you require?"

"Oh. Let's say large enough to feed a party of twelve. About ten kilos I think."

"Very good, Madame."

We left the butcher shop and walked up the steps through the crowded street, and back out the Jaffa Gate to our car. When we got into the car, Mom turned to me. "Josie," she said, "has it been so dreadful for you here, really? And am I such a lousy mother that you actually wanted to run away?"

"I wasn't running away from you, Mom. I was running back home."

"Sweetie, you can't very well run to something, without running away at the same time." She sighed and we sat there for a while. Then she turned the key in the ignition, and started the car. I mean, what could I say?

We drove home quietly. Past Lord Montefiore's Windmill and Yemin Moshe, past the road through the park that leads to Mishkanot, past the Khan and the railroad station, past Abu Tor.

The sun was setting, the quick twilight of the Middle East already luminous over the distant brooding hills. God, Jerusalem is beautiful!

23

$\mathcal{M}$om and I had a quiet dinner at home that evening. Afterwards we had a long talk about mothers and daughters in general, and me and her in particular. Also about men and women in general, and Mira and Grisha in particular.

"Don't you see," Mom said to me, "all the qualities that make Mira so lovely are bound to mean a great deal to Grisha. He must have been so lonely before he met her. And of course she missed Mr. Yanovitch so much. They need each other, Josie."

"I need Mira, too," I said stubbornly.

"Of course you do, honey, but not in the same way. You need Mira because she is warm and sweet and cozy and always there. Even when I'm not. But the fact is, Josie, you do have me. And though you might sometimes wish I were home more often when you need me, you can expect that I'll be around most of the time while you're growing up, and quite a while afterwards too. Because sweetie, I'm your mother, and I love you." She hugged me, and I hugged her back.

"Mira needs me as much as she needs Grisha," I said, not really believing it.

"Mira needs someone to be able to plan a future with," Mom said, gently stroking my hair. "Someone who will be part of her future. And because Grisha is so much part of her past, he can be a much fuller part of her future."

"How do you mean?" I said.

Mom had put a record on and Boris was part of our conversation, playing a Schubert Fantasia that kept weaving in and out. I felt very close to her. She and I and Boris's music were making nice patterns in my head.

"Well, sort of like when Mira was teaching you Moukha Tsokotoukha," Mom answered. "Every child in Russia knows Moukha from the time he's a baby. Moukha is part of growing up Russian, just like Yankee Doodle is part of growing up American. Mira could teach you Moukha, but she couldn't permeate your mind with all the elements that constitute a Russian childhood. Where just saying the word *Moukha* evokes all kinds of peculiarly Russian fantasies that come to life in your head complete and three dimensional."

We were sitting out on the balcony. A full moon was lighting the pale clay-colored hills before us, and the scent of roses and jasmine was heavy on the air. "Yes," Mom murmured into my hair, looking out towards the hills, "for all that I love this, all this powerful mystical beauty," she was talking so quietly, almost to herself, "it would mean more shared with someone who has heard the tinkle of ice in a pitcher of lemonade, and the slam of a screen door on the front porches of my childhood summer evenings."

"Does that mean that people from different places can't really get to love each other?" I asked drowsily, snuggled into her arms.

"Absolutely not." Mom shook her head vigorously. "It just means that when you get a little older it gets a lot harder to share your life with someone who has a radically different background. The older you get, the longer your past is. Mira isn't very young, sweetie, and everything here is terribly new to her. Think of how nice it must be for her to have someone who has memories of the same sights and sounds and smells that she has. Not to mention poems and politicians and platitudes."

"In some ways, that's how I feel," I said. "But I don't just want someone to share the memories of things back home with. I want to be home, to live at home again."

"Josie, I think what you really mean, though you haven't been able to say it even to yourself, is that you want home just as you knew it when you were a little girl. But honey, it's been two years since we first came here, and you've grown up tremendously during that time. You're not that little girl anymore."

I thought about what she said for a while. "Do you mean that I am trying to get back to being little again?" I asked.

"Not entirely," said Mom. "I think what you did with

Mira and Grisha and the puppets shows your independence, your wanting to grow up. But part of you doesn't want to give up being a little girl yet. And that's perfectly O.K. As long as you realize that going back to a house in Connecticut isn't going to make you a little girl again. You're really fighting very hard to grow up, Josie, and I'm afraid I haven't been much help lately. I guess if I were in a Best Mother competition, I'd score very low." She paused for a while and we listened to Boris. "You know, I think we probably will be going back to the US at the end of the school year," she said.

"You mean it?" I yelled. "Just for the summer or for good?"

"Let's take it from day to day, honey. I don't know for how long. Longer than the summer, most likely."

"You mean I'm going to go back to school in Connecticut?"

"I don't want to live in Connecticut again. I've heard a lot of nice things about Toronto."

"Mom, that's not even in the States!"

"Well, it's close. I think we'll go out to San Francisco for a while, and see what that's like."

"Why do we have to schlepp around to a million different places? Why can't we just settle down?"

Mom sighed. "Josie, I know it's terribly hard for you to understand, but I'm really not sure where I want to be, and I guess you'll just have to accept uncertainty for a while."

The record came to an end. The turntable stopped spinning, and the record player clicked itself off.

"What about Boris?"

"I don't know," Mom said. "That's one of the reasons I want to go back. You know, what I said about Mira and Grisha is true for me and Boris. His dreams are in Polish, Josie, not in Hebrew or English. Savagely tortured dreams of a boy just your age growing to adolescence in a concentration camp. Everything that happens between us has that in it. Everything." We sat there quietly, listening to the silence that had replaced Boris's music.

Mom got up and pulled me to my feet. "Come," she said. "Let's go over and see Mira. You can tell her how glad you are that she has Grisha."

"Mom, will I be able to visit Mira sometime? Will I get to come back and see her?"

"Of course you will, honey, we'll both come back and visit. How could I stay away from Jerusalem?"

"When? When will we come?"

"Hey! Hold it a minute! We haven't even left yet!" She looked at me. "You know, Josie, with all your kvetching, it's there for you too, isn't it? That feeling, almost like a secret singing in the blood. Jerusalem!"

Abu Rauchi was sitting in front of Mira's apartment house, a transistor radio to his ear. The plaintive wailing sound that was coming from the radio, endlessly long and all on one infinitely drawn-out note, is the pop standard of all the Arab watchmen on our street. Abu Rauchi was listening with obvious pleasure.

"It's like music to his ear," I said to Mom.

"It's lovely," said Abu Rauchi in Arabic, smiling and

inclining his head toward us in that very polite and formal way he has.

"Yes, it is in truth lovely," answered Mom in Hebrew.

When we got to Mira's landing, we could hear the sound of her accordian. She was playing Ivushka Zelenaya and singing the words very softly. As I was about to knock, she started to play the chorus, and a thin reedy voice joined hers. "It's Grisha," I whispered to Mom. "I don't want to go in."

"Don't be silly, Josie," Mom said. "You're just going to have to get used to the idea of Grisha and Mira together." She knocked on the door, and the singing stopped. Grisha opened the door, and held out his arms to me.

"Oh, it's the little Chassid," he said. "And her mother. It is so charming to make your acquaintance." He took Mom's hand in both of his own. "We missed you the night of the performance. I hope your sick friend is better."

Mom's eyebrows did their disappearing trick as she looked at me. "Yes," she said, "my friend is much better now. I'm sorry I missed the performance, too. But Josie tells me there will be another show in two weeks, and I certainly expect to attend it."

"It will be our pleasure," said Grisha.

Mira was bustling around with the tea kettle and cups, putting extra chairs around the kitchen table, and calling us to come sit. I ran over to her, threw my arms around her, and buried my face in her neck. She kissed the top of my head, and though she was holding a teacup in each hand, she managed to hug me.

"Oh Mira," I said softly, so that only she could hear. "I am glad that you have Grisha and that you won't be all alone anymore and that when you say Moukha you both remember birthday parties with samovars where the buildings all have onion-shaped domes and that the music you hear is the same music that he hears and that when you look at the paperweight I gave you and it starts snowing you both see it snowing in Moscow, and the cold and the ice are the cold and the ice of a Russian winter!"

Mira looked delighted when I backed away from her and sat down. She patted my shoulder lovingly, and said something to Grisha.

"Mira says she used to have to bend down to kiss the top of your head, but now she almost has to stand on tip-toes to kiss you!"

"Yes, Josie has grown quite a bit lately," said Mom.

Mira was obviously bursting with wanting to tell us her news. She got her shopping bag, and pulled out a little crepe-paper party basket which she carefully set in front of me. Then she set another one just as carefully in front of Mom.

"Ani rotsa," she said slowly in Hebrew, "l'hasmin . . ."

Grisha put his hand over hers and gently interrupted her.

"Anakhnu rotsim, we want," he said. "The two of us, plural."

"Ken, ken," she smiled and then threw her hands up in the air and said the whole thing quickly in Russian.

"We want to invite you to a party," said Grisha. "We are going to get married and we want all our friends to join us in a celebration."

"Oh, how absolutely lovely!" said Mom as though she had never suspected anything of the sort. She got up and hugged and kissed Mira, and I got up and hugged and kissed Mira, and Mira pulled me down on her lap.

She was saying something about coming to Israel, and about Mr. Yanovitch, and she started to cry, just a little bit, using the corner of her apron to wipe away the tears; but she was smiling all the time, so I didn't really need Grisha to tell me what she said. But he told Mom anyway. "Mira says that Josie has been her dearest and best companion, and that without Josie she never would have found her feet here in Israel so quickly, especially after the death of Mr. Yanovitch."

Mom looked over at me and smiled. "Josie is a dear," she said. "I am glad she has been such a good friend to Mira. But you know, Mira has been a good friend to Josie, too. They found good friends in each other when they both needed friends. I am so glad that Mira has you now, and I know Josie is happy that when we leave, Mira won't be alone."

"You are leaving?" asked Grisha.

"Yes," said Mom, "I think we will probably be going back to the States when the school year is over."

"Ah, then we have yet a little time. Perhaps you will change your mind," said Grisha.

"No, no, I don't think so," said Mom.

Just this once I think Mira must have understood everything Mom said. She lifted my chin up, and looked into my face. "Ken?" she asked me. "Ze nakhun?" "Yes? Is this right?" I threw my arms around her neck.

"Ken," I answered, trying to bury my sobs in her shoulder. "But I'll come visit you Mira, honest I will!"

24

"Roses are red, Violets are blue, If I looked like you, I'd be a Jew," Maryanne wrote on the pale pink page in my autograph book. "You don't mind, do you Josie?" she asked, drawing flowers and curlicues all around the poem.

"No. Why should I mind," I answered.

Funny about it though.

"What do you expect?" Boris had said to Mom when she told him about Mathias and Mrs. Farrell. "Out of all the schools in Jerusalem you had to choose a goyishe school. You come to Israel, where finally you're not in the minority, and what do you do? You put Josie in a school where she's probably the only Jewish kid. I bet even where you come from, in that small town in the States, she wasn't the only Jew."

"It had nothing to do with her being Jewish," Mom

said. "Besides, she's not the only Jewish kid in this school either."

"Nu, so what does that prove? Only that there are other meshuganis!"

Maryanne finished coloring a flower red. She drew a heart carefully around the whole design and wrote her name on the bottom of the page. Then she gave my autograph book to Rosamunda, and Rosamunda gave hers to me. I wasn't the only one leaving at the end of the week. Rosamunda's father was being transferred to Paris. "A step down, really. Daddy says all the big news is right here in the Middle East. And we are all going to miss that super Shabbat lunch they serve at the American Colony. It's buffet, you know. You can go back for more as often as you like, and it doesn't cost the world, either. But actually, Mummy and I are looking forward to Paris because it's so close to home."

Home. Home for Rosamunda is a small house in St. John's Wood, with Mum and Dad and baby brother, all snug and smug and roly-poly. I wonder where home will be for me. With Mom. On the East Coast? The West Coast? In Toronto?

"That's right," I said to Rosamunda. "Close to jars and jars of Marmite and all those gorgeously sensible woolens brought to you by Marks and Sparks."

Rosamunda's pale gray eyes looked at me briefly, but she didn't say anything.

"Thank Gawd I'm not leaving," said Maryanne. "I'd curl up and die if I had to go back for good. I mean I do like to visit England and all, but Jerusalem is home to me. I love it here."

We were sitting under a eucalyptus tree during recess. Carlos had just invited us to a party at his house. He was going back to Costa Rica in the fall. "It's not going to be any fun here next year," cried Maryanne in mock despair. Very simple. Very clear. Jerusalem is home for Maryanne. It is not home for me.

"Don't worry, Maryanne. I'll still be here," said Stella. "My father will be ambassador for a long time." Stella's father is the ambassador from Colombia. The embassy is in a fancy building a few blocks from school. The other day Stella asked me to walk over there with her to get some money from her father so we could go into town. The big Mercedes parked in front of the building had the same official state emblem on it as the plaque on the wrought-iron balcony. Next to the plaque the ambassador had hung his socks out to dry. "Papa always does his laundry over here," Stella said matter of factly. "He likes to have clean socks when he goes out to all those official cocktail parties. He says his feet don't swell up when he stands around drinking if his socks are clean."

"How come he doesn't bring a clean pair from home?" I asked.

Stella opened her eyes wide. "I guess he never thought of that," she said. "Besides, he has nothing else to do all day."

As long as Stella's father is comfortably installed in the embassy, with loads of free time to do his laundry, Jerusalem will be home for Stella. But not for me. O Jerusalem, I love you . . . love you.

Jenine El Gazi came over and sat down with us. "I think everyone ought to bring something to Carlos's party," she said. "You know, like we could all chip in and get a cake or something."

"I have a better idea," said Maryanne. "Why don't we go over to City Grocery this afternoon and get a whole lot of candy. They told my Mum that they were expecting a shipment of sweets from America and England."

"Sweets from America?" asked Rosamunda, her eyes lighting up. "Ohhh, maybe they'll have Reese's peanut butter cups." She moaned ecstatically, hugging herself and licking her lips.

Things had been very nice for me at school for several weeks. Mathias hadn't really pestered me since the day Mom came in to see Mrs. Farrell. Actually, he gave me these terrible dirty looks whenever he passed me, but he didn't do anything to me. He sort of gazed heavenward after he had looked at me, and his lips started moving fast. Maybe he was saying the Lord's Prayer.

Somehow, even without a bra, Mom was able to convince Mrs. Farrell that I wasn't the troublemaker. Mom got a short note of apology the day after she saw her. The note said somewhat enigmatically that Mrs. Farrell felt that she had been to blame for the "unsatisfactory nature of the interview, which was in part due to my intolerance." Mom and I puzzled over that for a long time. Intolerance of what? My occasional tattiness? Of Mom's (to Mrs. Farrell's way of thinking) eccentric clothing and hairstyle? Or her intolerance of unfettered bosoms? The handwriting looked just like Mrs. Farrell. Prim, exaggeratedly neat, and perfectly straight. No kinkiness of any sort.

But actually, it wasn't just that Mathias no longer persecuted me. It was because suddenly I was being included in lots of things. Like Carlos's party, and Stella asking me to go into town with her and all.

I knew it had nothing to do with me in any way though. I mean, even if Mom said I'd grown up quite a bit, I still didn't have my period, and my shirts didn't look any different in the front than they did before.

It was really because Maryanne was so popular. Anyone that Maryanne was friendly with just naturally got included in everything. That goes for all kinds of other things too. Like take the puppet show. Mira and Grisha and I were scheduled to put on another performance at the Youth Club, and Mom thought it would be a good idea if I gave my share of the money we earned to Mira, so she could buy a really nice wedding present, something she really wanted.

"The only thing is," I said, "we haven't had time to put together a new show. We're doing the old one over again. All Mira's classmates from the Ulpan and all Grisha's friends from Moadon Rasco have seen that one. I don't know how much of an audience we can pick up just from the parade. It's not as though we'll be advertising something new."

"Why don't you put up a sign at school," Mom said. "There's quite a large potential audience there."

"I suppose you're right," I said doubtfully. "But do you think they'd like a puppet show about a little Chassid?"

"A puppet show is a puppet show," said Mom. "Besides, look at what a long run *Fiddler on the Roof* had."

When I told Maryanne about it she got all excited. "Let's sell tickets in advance at school," she said. "That way, you'll know beforehand the minimum you can expect. Anything you pick up from the people who walk in off the street will be that much extra."

She and Jenine made tickets out of colored paper and sold them all off. Jenine has a brother in one of the lower forms, and he took care of that end of it, while Maryanne got all her friends to buy the rest. Practically our whole class was there the night of the performance. Even Catherine had somehow managed to get her father to allow her to come, and when I peeked out from behind the crepe-paper curtain before the show, I saw her sitting in the front row next to Mom.

"Oy vai voy," said Grisha, before stepping out in front of the puppet theatre to explain the show. "I haven't seen so many goyim since I left Moscow."

But the show didn't really need any explaining. Mom was right. The little Chassid and his teacher were familiar enough caricatures of the mischievous pupil and his poor bedeviled teacher, to keep the audience laughing from beginning to end.

After the show, Mira and Grisha and I went to Café Atara again, and this time Mom came with us. Somehow though, I didn't enjoy the ice-cream sundae I ordered any better than I had the last time.

"What's the matter, Josie?" Mom asked after watching me mush it around in the dish. "Are you tired after all the excitement tonight?"

I looked down at the limp strawberries floating in thin syrup. "No, it isn't that," I said, carefully dripping syrup over a bald spot on the ice cream. "It's just that I've been remembering all the times Mira and I have had together. All the cups of tea with strawberry preserves that I drank with her. All the times I've listened to her sing Ivushka Zelenaya. How she loves to hear me say Moukha Tsoko-toukha because she says I pronounce the word *Moukha* with so much tenderness. How much she laughs at my little Chassid, no matter how often she has seen him do the same dumb things. How much she loves to watch it snow on the little houses in my paperweight."

My voice had been getting thicker and thicker. I sat there looking down, not seeing anything but my hand holding the spoon that was dripping strawberry syrup over vanilla ice cream, and the tip of my nose that was getting larger and larger, and redder and redder. Now a drop formed on the end of it and trembled there, perilously close to falling into the ice cream.

"Douzhynka." Mira's hand came over and covered mine.

Mom passed a tissue to me. I blew my nose, and lifted my eyes to Mira. Her blue eyes were looking at me, brimming with tears. Oh Mira, I'm going to miss you so much!

25

Boris came to say good-bye to us the night before we left. "It's not really good-bye," Mom said, gently shoving Khumie away. "I'll be back to visit, and Josie will too."

Khumie came into my room, and prowled around the boxes and debris. "Mom," I yelled, "get Khumie out of here, I can't finish packing."

"He doesn't want you to go," called Boris. "You see how smart he is!" All our voices seemed oddly wrong, echoing off the stone walls of the living room and hallway. Already the place had a vacant-house sound. Khumie picked up my teddy bear and started to walk out.

"Give, give," I said. "Drat it, you stupid dog. How come you don't speak English? Ten li, ten li miyad, kelev tov!" Khumie came over, teddy bear in mouth, wagging his tail when he heard the Hebrew. He dropped Teddy at my feet. I stuffed him into a canvas book bag that would be carry-on luggage, and surveyed the room.

None of the furniture was ours. Only the throw pillows, the Arab tapestries, the baskets, and all the odds and ends we had accumulated still had to be packed into boxes to be picked up by the shipping agent tomorrow. My books had been sent already, and the heavy stuff like the rocks I'd collected. "What's this, rocks?" the man who had come for them had grumbled, as he staggered under the weight of the box.

"Oh Josie," Mom said. "When are you going to learn to travel light?"

I probably never will. I guess I'll never be a real traveller. It's very difficult for me to throw away the clothes I've outgrown. I know Mom's going to yell at me when she finds out how much overweight we are tomorrow. I hope she doesn't make a scene at the check-in counter. I mean she's probably right when she says five suitcases full of old T-shirts and blue jeans that are too small for me is really overdoing it. I sat on a bulging suitcase, and tried to get the zipper to zip.

"Why don't you let me drive you to Lod tomorrow," Boris was saying. "You're being very silly."

"I've already told you. It's better this way. I hate long-drawn-out good-byes. Besides, the whole thing at Lod is a terrible drag. It would be anticlimactic. You can pick up the car later in the day. Here's the extra key."

"I still don't understand why you have to run away in the middle."

"That's just it. What's the middle for you, may be the end for me."

"You're a very strange woman."

"Not strange. Just terribly American."

The wake-up service wakes us up at quarter to four. The last time I'll be awakened in Hebrew. "Boker tov," says the voice. "Ha sha'ah shalosh arbaim v'hamesh." We get out of bed and dress, foggy with sleep. There is already a faint hint of light in the sky when I look out through the sliding door to the balcony. The hills lie quietly pale and mysterious. Mom has coffee, and I have the last of the milk and some toast. Then Mom turns off the refrigerator, and washes up.

The bell rings. It is Grisha and Mira, come over to help carry the luggage down. We follow them, and stand ineffectually around. Abu Rauchi comes out of the bomb shelter in Mira's building, dapper as ever, his kaffiyeh very white against the deep deep blue of the dawn sky. No one says anything much. Abu Rauchi wants to know when we will be back, and shakes his head sorrowfully when he understands that we are not coming back. He pats me on the head as I stand there shivering in the cool damp air.

Grisha piles as much luggage as he can in the trunk, the rest on the luggage rack. "I can't understand it," Mom says. "How come we have twelve pieces of luggage?" She is just saying it to fill in the silence really. Grisha doesn't say anything except for an occasional grunt when he hoists a particularly heavy suitcase into place.

Mira says nothing at all. She has on a pink bathrobe and kibbutz house slippers. They are old fashioned, tan, brown, and black fuzzy plaid that come up to her ankles.

She seems shorter than she did the first time I saw her, the day I watched from my window as she moved in. Shorter and rounder. Her face is rosy from sleep, her short silky white hair a tufted halo around her head. She stands a little to one side, holding the top of the bathrobe together at the throat.

Finally, Grisha gets everything arranged.

"Why don't you sit in the back, Josie," Mom says. "You'll be able to catch a nap on the way to the airport."

"O.K.," I mumble, not looking at Mira. I have taken Teddy out of the book bag, and hold him under my arm. The book bag itself I refuse to give up, even though it is heavy and dragging me down. It has all my neatsies in it. An extra special shell from Eilat, all fluted and pearly pink. A tiny piece of a Roman column that I picked up in Caesarea. My Caran D'Ache in case I feel like drawing on the plane. All the makeup—the blush-on and eye shadow and lip gloss—that Maryanne and Stella gave me as a going-away present. My comb and brush and mirror. A tiny little bottle of perfume. The nested dolls Mira gave me. My diary, and all the journals that I kept here. The copy of Moukha that Mira gave me after I learned to say it without any mistakes. My autograph book.

"Lehitra'ot," says Abu Rauchi shaking my hand. "Lehitra'ot, Geverit," he bows to Mom.

"Good-bye, little Chassid," says Grisha, kissing me first on one cheek, then on the other. "Good-bye, Leila," he says to Mom, kissing her cheeks too.

I turn to Mira. It is very quiet except for the wind that has come up with the dawn. Her little round figure stands sharply etched against the pale hills and the sky which is beginning to brighten in the east. The cool wind ruffles her hair around her face and flaps the pink bathrobe against her legs. She lets go of the bathrobe, where she's been clutching it, and stretches her arms out to me. "Douzhynka," she whispers.

"Oh Mira, Mira!" I cry. I drop Teddy and the book bag, and run into her arms.

We drive down past the Israel Museum, past the white gleam of the dome that houses the Dead Sea Scrolls. It is still dark enough for everything in this pale gold city to be light against the sky as we turn left at the Paz station where a line of soldiers are already waiting for a tramp. Mom pulls up. "Macomb bishvil achad le Lod," she says. "Room for one to Lod."

The soldier, red haired and tired looking, puts his pack into the back of the car, and gets into the front, cradling his Uzi on his lap.

"Amerikait?" he asks.

"Yes," Mom answers and we lapse into silence.

The sky is pale and pearly as we round the curve where the entrance to the cemetery where Mr. Yanovitch is buried forks off to the left. It is pretty much downhill now. The highway out of Jerusalem is one long drop, except for a steep stretch where the car labors to climb, only to plunge downward in long curves again. We pass Moza Illit, pass the turnoff for Abu Gosh. The hills, at first skeletal in the gray light, are beginning to be fully contoured. The ancient terraces are like vertebrae; they keep the clay-colored earth from falling, falling into the deep wadis.

All around now the sky is lighter, a translucent blue. We pass Shar Ha Gai, the old British stronghold, pass the monastery, golden in the early morning, and the turnoff for Ramallah. Suddenly Mom begins to cry. She drives around the sharp bend in the road to the right, and over the narrow bridge marked NARROW BRIDGE in Hebrew, Arabic, and English, and her shoulders are shaking and tears are streaming down her face.

The soldier sitting next to her looks at her. He shifts his Uzi, so that his left hand is free, and touches her gently on the shoulder. "Yi hieh biseder," he says, his large eyes soft and earnest.

I lean over the back of her seat and pat her. "It's all right, Mom," I say. "It's all right." The tears start up in my eyes, blinding me so that I can't see the hills anymore, the gaunt tawny hills of Jerusalem that I love so much. I sit there weeping weeping weeping as we drive into the fertile plain before us, green under the bright blue sky of morning. "I'll come back," I sob softly. "I'll come back."

❦

26

❦

The girl at the check-in counter smiled up at me. She was bending over one of my open suitcases, riffling through blue jeans and underwear. A pair of shocking pink G-string bikinis that Stella had given me fell out. Mom's eyebrows disappeared.

"Ot Amerikait? You're American?" asked the girl. "Does your suitcase look as it did when you packed it? Did anyone give you something to take for them? Did you buy anything in the Old City in the past few days?"

"No," I answered.

"All right. You can close the suitcase now. Have a pleasant journey. Shalom, ve lehitra'ot."

Mom and I fumbled around trying to jam everything back into the last suitcase. The zipper was definitely stuck.

"Damn it, Josie. Why did you have to pack all this junk," Mom said.

"Here, let me help," a cool, accented voice said. About forty, I decided, giving him a quick once-over. Hair starting to thin at the top; he's compensating by having it longer in the back. He was very slender and distinguished looking, his corduroy jacket thrown casually over his shoulder. Mom was smiling at him, not flirty; Mom never flirts. Just openly interested.

"He probably isn't in the arts," I could almost hear her saying to herself. "Too bad." Mom has a thing about talent. I mean real talent, not just people who play around at self-discovery. This guy looked fringy though. An art historian maybe? A musicologist? Anyhow, he was deftly closing my suitcase and asking Mom at the same time if she'd like to have coffee with him in the upstairs restaurant after he'd checked through.

It turned out he was an art critic.

"An art critic?"

"Yes, for an Australian newspaper." That's how come the accent. Mom and he chatted constantly. They knew some of the same people, both in Israel and New York, where it turned out he was going to be for three months. How fortunate.

They talked on and on. We went through body security check, got our boarding passes, went into the waiting lounge. He carried Mom's carry-on luggage for her as well as his own, although Mom's was terribly heavy. I saw him wince when he picked it up. He didn't offer to carry my canvas book bag, with Teddy's head and paws sticking out over the top.

I sat down a few seats away from them. The beginning-of-an-affair chitchat really gets on my nerves. I looked in my book bag just to make sure I had everything, and got out the makeup Maryanne and Stella gave me and my mirror.

I put on a little of the lip gloss, pouting into the mirror the way I'd seen Stella do it. Then I caught the reflection of a face smiling at me in the mirror. God, was he cute! About sixteen or seventeen, curly blond hair, blue eyes, smiling at me in the mirror! I put the makeup away carefully, got up, and walked slowly into the ladies' room. Back very straight, just swaying my hips ever so gently, like they're on greased ball bearings, the way Mom does.

Once I got into the ladies' room, I fluffed my hair up quickly, pinched my cheeks until they were all rosy, used some spit to flatten down my eyebrows, which are growing in frizzy from being pulled out so often, and ran my tongue over my lips to make the lip gloss shinier. Then I walked out.

He was waiting for me just outside the door to the ladies' room.

"Bonjour!" he said, taking hold of both my hands. He leaned back a little, and swung my hands back and forth, looking at me and smiling. He was so cute, all I could do was smile, smile, smile.

"Oh," he said. "Vous êtes jolie. Vous êtes belle!"

"Flight 001, Tel Aviv to Paris and New York now boarding at Gate Three," said the voice on the loud speaker. "Flight 001, Tel Aviv to Paris and New York now boarding."

Format by Kohar Alexanian
Set in 12 pt. Baskerville
Composed, printed and bound by Vail-Ballou Press, Inc.
HARPER & ROW, PUBLISHERS, INCORPORATED

Temple Israel

Minneapolis, Minnesota

In Honor of the Bat Mitzvah of
WENDY GRACEMAN
By Her Parents,
Mr. & Mrs. Barry Graceman

October 15, 1977